Runaway Princess Bride

Runaway Princess Bride

A Castles of Dallas Romance

LENORA WORTH

TULE
PUBLISHING

Dedication

To all of the Cinderellas out there. You don't need a tiara, darling. Buy the shoes instead!

Dear Reader,

I enjoyed going along on this adventure with Aidan and Cara. They come from two different worlds which is what made them so fascinating to me. Cara wanted to do the right things for all the wrong reasons. Aidan saw the good behind her facade. But he was hiding behind his own facade, too. It took a con artist to make them remove their masks and find an honest love.

I hope you have enjoyed this series. That theme of facades and masks followed me throughout these books. But seriously, it was all about the shoes for me. We're told to always put our best foot forward. I hope the three heroines in this book did just that by stepping out of their facades to find men who could keep up with them and love them for their strengths and for their weaknesses. We all had a blast, that's for sure!

Chapter One

A N ALARM SHRIEKED through the cold December night. The loud deafening noise sounded like a banshee as Aidan Castle pulled his Jeep into to the garage at the Double L Ranch.

He and Johnny Darrow, head of security at Castle Department Store, had been in charge of setting up a state-of-the-art security system at the secluded Fort Worth ranch owned by Nico Lamon and named after his mother Lila Lamon.

Stepping out of the black Jeep, Aidan glanced around while he hurried to check the alarm, the chilly night air hitting him with a zing. No one in sight. The new system still needed some tweaking, so he might have triggered something.

He'd reached the garage keypad to disarm it when the alarm stopped and the night went silent.

His cell buzzed. The alarm company calling to check.

Aidan answered and identified himself. "I think I triggered something when I opened the garage door. We're still working out the kinks. I'll call back if I need you."

He started inside, his hand on the doorknob into the hallway off the back of the kitchen, when he heard a scream,

1

followed by loud laughter. Kids?

Or a woman, maybe?

Waiting a couple of beats, Aidan stayed still. Maybe he should have let the alarm company send the sheriff out.

Glancing around, he looked for a weapon. All the guns were locked up in the gun cabinet in Nico's office inside the house.

When he spotted a big wrench lying on a worktable, he grabbed it. Carefully opening the door, he silently slipped into the big, dark kitchen. Nothing out of the ordinary there. Outside, the wind picked up. A winter storm cloaked the night with threats of bad weather.

Aidan would worry about that later. Right now, he had to find out whom or what had tripped that alarm.

Then he saw the empty champagne bottle on the counter and a wineglass with a bright red lipstick stain on its rim.

Definitely a woman.

Okay. How to proceed?

Aidan moved from the kitchen to the big den across the hall, his Doc Martens making very little noise, his eyes adjusting to the muted light.

He came around the tan leather sectional, the heavy wrench raised, and stopped in a quiet skid. There, face-down on the couch like a fallen flower, lay a woman wearing a wedding dress.

Aidan had never encountered anything like this, and he wasn't in the mood for games on this cold Wednesday night. Tired after a long day at the site of the latest Castle endeavor, a high-tech digital and electronics store located at a new tech complex not far from the ranch, he only wanted a sandwich and some sleep.

The creature on the couch let out a soft moan that sounded like the last of her sobs.

Putting the wrench down on a table, he walked over and stared at her. She was breathing, her back moving against the pearls that glistened down the high-necked sleeveless wedding dress. Dark copper-streaked hair shimmered in the muted glow from the backyard security light shining through the windows on the other side of the room.

Not sure if he should poke her or call out, Aidan bent down and pushed a thick strand of her hair off her face.

The woman groaned and lifted a hand to slap at him, hitting ineffectively into the air. "Go away."

"Hey," Aidan said, something in her voice tapping on a nerve. "Hey, who are you and why are you here?"

She groaned and lifted her head, her eyes going from two slits to two round, surprised orbs. "You."

"You," Aidan echoed, still kneeling beside her, the scent of her shampoo now on his fingers.

Cara Lamon, Nico's younger sister, lifted on her elbows to stare at him with big luminous gray eyes that spoke volumes.

The last time they'd seen each other had been the day after the Wild West Costume Ball at the Lone Star Castle store three months ago. That night, even though they rubbed each other the wrong way in so many ways, they'd both had too much champagne, followed by too many stolen kisses in a quiet corner.

When they'd finally stopped making out, she'd stared up at Aidan with those stormy-gray eyes and said, "I'm sorry. I'm secretly engaged."

Then she'd left the party.

The next morning, she'd come downstairs from a guest room at the estate, only to find the whole family celebrating his sister Annabelle's newfound happiness with none other than Johnny Darrow. Cara had taken one look at Aidan before turning to head back upstairs.

Apparently, she was the kiss-and-run type. The same type who'd teased him and mocked him in high school.

She'd hightailed a beeline out of Texas in a big hurry, obviously heading back to Italy to plan her secret marriage.

So why was she now here wearing a wedding dress?

CARA LAMON'S NIGHTMARE continued. She could see it all so clearly in her mind. Her doubts had made her question her fiancé. Her lawyer had done some asking around, discreetly hiring a private investigator. He didn't like what he'd found so he'd talked her into creating a prenup to be sure. She'd already given Trey part of the money for his charity—all done with full transparency and following the routine protocol—so why the rush to get married? The lawyer told her a prenup would either seal the deal or the groom would balk and walk away with the money he already had. Lamon Foundation money, part of which she'd transferred into a holding account. She'd found it distasteful to ask for a prenuptial agreement and yet ... she needed to know if Trey loved her or only wanted her money.

So many times, she'd been infatuated and then she'd balked and run away before things went any further. Trey had been the first man to get her to the altar. Almost.

She could see herself standing in her wedding gown, her hair caught up in crystal clips, her shoes white satin Lamon pumps with the famous scrolled black L on the sole and sparkling crystal flowers across the toebox.

That nightmare had happened an hour before the wedding, after she'd finished getting dressed. A secret wedding, an elopement of sorts. Romantic and very exclusive. He wanted her all to himself, no cameras and no nosy family or friends. When her lawyer had explained the prenup to Trey, he'd balked, accusing her of not trusting him. She'd never seen him so angry. Then they'd talked, and he'd convinced her that he loved her and they didn't need paperwork. They belonged together. They'd kissed, and ... the whole prenup thing had seemed silly. But she'd suddenly realized the wedding would be a big mistake. Like the others, he only wanted her money and status.

Which made her feel like the worse kind of fool since Trey had mentioned the other half of the money he needed. Urgently. For the orphans in Botswana. Was she so pathetic and desperate she could fall for a smooth-talking, good-looking Lothario even after she'd been so careful? Her head said yes. Her heart said no. Trey loved her, didn't he?

Even so, she'd turned the tables on Trey Wellington and all his claims of a royal British lineage that dated back to

King Alfred himself. After asking Trey to come to her suite for one last kiss before the wedding so he could see her in her beautiful dress and somehow be honest with her, she'd left the lawyer to greet him at the altar while she'd hopped a private jet straight to Texas. With cake and champagne on board. She couldn't marry him. It wasn't about signing contracts or who had the most money. It was about falling in love and knowing she could trust the other person. She'd withheld telling her mother and brother about Trey, which meant she hadn't been thinking clearly. Had Trey manipulated her and charmed her to the point that she couldn't make a rational decision?

She'd come back to her favorite place to clear her head and try to get over her heartache.

Now, she was having another nightmare. Aidan Castle kneeled beside her, that inky tuft of black bangs hanging over his winged brows with a rebel attitude that made her remember how he'd kissed her at the costume ball. Kissed her over and over. And she'd liked it. But she'd been engaged at the time, and … she wouldn't be unfaithful to Trey.

Trey the betrayer. Trey, who even now was probably trying to woo another clueless socialite. Trey, whose kisses didn't feel quite the same after she'd kissed Aidan.

When would she ever learn that men could not be trusted? Hadn't her own father taught her that lesson?

Right now, however, Trey wasn't her problem. The man staring at her with those charcoal eyes was. This man she'd thought about way too much since that crazy kissing night. This quiet, brooding man had made her doubt herself and her need to hurry and get married.

The one man she didn't need to see sat staring at her like a hawk about to attack a dove.

"Aidan, the high-tech prince," she said with a still-drunk grin. "I need more champagne."

She lifted and twisted toward sitting, satin crinkling all around her like brittle ice, her eyes misting in spite of her refusal to cry anymore. "Guess what? I didn't get married."

Holding up one of her exquisite white satin Lamon pumps with the dainty crystal-embossed flowers sprayed across the vamp, he nodded. "That's obvious since I didn't find your groom hovering around anywhere," he said, standing to find a seat on a nearby ottoman. "So what happened, Cara who kisses in corners?"

No sympathy. The man sometimes came across like a machine.

Except when he kissed her. Nothing mechanical about his lips. They worked just fine.

The imprint of his kisses had made her doubt her plans to get married. And that doubt had gone deep beyond the surface. Her instincts had hinted that she'd rushed into this romantic, secret elopement with a man she didn't really know.

Maybe because she'd longed for love and Trey had offered it and the world, too?

Humiliated, she lashed out at Aidan. "What are *you* doing in my house?"

"*Your* house?" He pushed at those enticing bangs, shooting her a winning smile. "It's called the Double L—for Lila

Lamon. Remember?"

"How can I forget?" she said, her own hair falling around her face, deflated and flat in the same way she felt. Then she sat straight up. "Oh, no. Aidan, my brother and mother think I'm in Bali on a special project. Trey and I … we were going to Bali for our honeymoon. They didn't know about the marriage. And I'd like to keep it that way."

He lifted one long leg and folded it across the other knee, his jeans nice and worn, his Doc Martens broken in. "Why did you go to such lengths to keep this non-marriage a secret?"

"I told Annabelle and you," she said, wishing she hadn't drunk that whole bottle of champagne after eating too much wedding cake. Wishing she'd never kissed him or told him her big secret. But he'd been rude to her that night, which made kissing him to get even the best kind of revenge.

Only, that notion had backfired in a big boom of attraction. Instead of hurrying away, he'd tugged her into his arms and returned the kiss. Two or three times.

"We don't count," Aidan said to her admission. "But Nico won't be happy, and you know your mom would have wanted to be at your wedding."

"He speaks the truth," she said, awe in her words, her arms crossed since she'd suddenly gone into a chill. "You actually care?"

"I didn't say that." Heading to the fireplace, he worked with a starter and twigs to get a fire going. "Why don't you get a shower and I'll cook us some food?"

"Do I smell?" she asked, sniffing her dress.

Her beautiful off-the-rack Lamon dress, high-necked and sleeveless, dainty, feminine, and channeling Jackie O.

Suddenly, she couldn't breathe. She had to get out of this wedding gown.

"Aidan?"

He turned. "What?"

"Help me." She tried to pry the tiny pearl buttons away, her fingers dragging at her back, her breath coming out in big gulps now. She couldn't wait. After foolishly keeping the dress on so she could hurry away, now she only wanted it off her body. "Aidan, please."

He came running as she ripped the back of the dress, pearl buttons scattering all over the big rug in front of the sofa.

His hands stilled on her shoulders. "Cara?"

"I have to change." Holding the dress up with her hands pressed against her chest, she ran out of the room, her heart breaking and ripping like the now-ruined gown.

Tears streaming down her face, Cara vowed to never fall in love again. Especially with the man who'd kissed her months ago and had now witnessed her meltdown.

Chapter Two

CARA RUSHED INTO her old bedroom upstairs, the scent of magnolia blossom candles reminding her of how much she loved the blooms in the spring. But winter chilled the house. Her room hadn't changed. Still muted florals with gold and white shimmering accent pieces. Lila had the house freshened and repainted every few years so it stayed clean and welcoming.

Good bones, her mother always said.

Lila had always told her children, "If you get in trouble, go home to Texas. Texas heals all wounds."

"I'm here, Mother," Cara said, her heart empty and cold like this house. "Here, alone, I thought. But … what should I do about Aidan?"

Her bedroom, one of two up here along with another den she and Nico had called theirs. She touched a hand to the quilted blue floral comforter on the tester bed that matched the bluish-white of the walls, turned on the light in the stark white bathroom, and gasped at the mascara stains on her face and the strands of hair curling toward her bare shoulders. And her dress. Ruined, torn, tattered. She'd literally ripped it off her body, her back now exposed.

Aidan must think she'd gone mad.

Well, in a way, she had. After a few half-hearted dating games with men who moved in the world of money and power and knew how to use both, Trey had been everything she'd ever dreamed about. She'd fallen hard. It had always been easy for her to become smitten, but she'd fallen in love with Trey.

Not sure if she'd needed the attention since her brother and mother were all wrapped up in their union with the mighty Castles, or if she'd always needed the attention because her own powerful, now-deceased father had mostly ignored her and moved on to the many models he'd had on the side. Cara realized something within her felt very insecure. But she was pushing her late twenties. Time to buckle up, buttercup.

Her overly protective brother always did extensive background checks—one reason her attempts at dating never had happy endings—so once Nico had come to Texas and become too busy to worry about her, she'd kept her new love a secret to show her defiance if nothing else. That and how Trey made her believe the paparazzi would hound them because of their notoriety. She'd never heard of him and he had her convinced he demanded privacy because he was related to the Queen of England. He had very impressive papers to back that up, too.

After having him thoroughly vetted, Cara imagined being introduced to Princess Kate, who occasionally visited The House of Lamon, and Meghan, the American actress married to a prince. Too many stars in her eyes.

Maybe she'd read one too many romance novels, but despite her parent's weird divorced-but-still-in-love oh-so-continental arrangement, she believed in romance and happy endings. Trey had promised her both while he'd wooed her into giving him a huge partial donation for his charity.

Nico would be so angry.

Mother would be so devastated.

Cara couldn't feel any lower than she did at this moment.

But … Aidan was here, and he seemed reasonable. He hadn't insulted her too badly or glared at her in that bored, condescending way. Well, maybe once or twice.

She'd much prefer that to his pity, however.

They'd gotten off on the wrong foot when they'd met at Castle's downtown store a few months ago. Then he'd been forced to give her a ride to the airport while he still had jet lag.

That ride had not gone well. The traffic, the heat, the country music drawling on the radio. Nothing worked. Each time she spoke, he made a sarcastic remark. Each time he spoke—when he did speak—she'd managed to say something incredibly snappish and snobbish.

"Do you like Dallas better than Milan?"

"Is there really a comparison?" she'd retorted before singing along with Toby Keith's "Red Solo Cup".

"I'll take that as a no."

"I like the Double L, but Texas is not Europe."

"Amen to that."

"You think I'm a spoiled snob."

"Amen to that."

And so on and so on.

Painful.

Next, the night of the Wild West Costume Ball at the new store at the Lone Star Shops…

She'd purposely dressed up as Annie Oakley, full of fire and spunkiness. He'd come walking up dressed in black like a gambler, his eyes grabbing hold of her with a bored dare.

Maybe it had been the domino masques they'd been required to wear, but something came over Cara and a bottle of champagne later, the insults had turned to kisses during another Toby Keith song—"You Shouldn't Kiss Me Like This".

She now had a love/hate relationship with Toby Keith.

She could no longer listen to beautiful classical music or even her favorite dance numbers. She'd become fascinated with the music she'd hated growing up. Those somebody-done-somebody-wrong songs actually held a lot of emotion and truth.

Aidan loved country music.

It didn't help that the Toby Keith song looped through her mind each time she thought of Aidan. She shouldn't have kissed him like that.

And he shouldn't have ever kissed her back.

Cara went to the big closet where she kept some casual clothes. She found some worn jeans and a long gray V-neck sweater, then she showered and damp-dried her hair, her face finally clear of old mascara. Throwing on an old T-shirt, she tossed the sweater over that, tugged on her jeans, and grabbed a pair of battered Frye ankle boots.

Putting on some pink gloss and a little smudge of smoky eye shadow she found from her stay here a few months ago, she deemed herself human enough to go back and face Aidan. She'd be polite to him when she told him he had to leave.

When she hit the stairs, a wonderful smell wafted through the house. Cara hurried through the wide hallway and into the big kitchen.

"Are you a chef?"

He glanced around, his gaze adjusting to her wearing little makeup and ratty clothes. She thought she saw a trace of appreciation before he looked away.

"I like to cook," he admitted. He'd pulled off his navy sweater, and now wore a black long-sleeved Henley that showed off his nice biceps and toned abs. "Annabelle and I used to hang out in the kitchen at the Castle estate. The chef taught us how to fend for ourselves since he noticed we kind of did that anyway."

Cara couldn't imagine that. Even with a trained staff, her mother still cooked and watched over Nico and Cara, protective and loving but allowing them to find their own ways, too. Cara always had food put in front of her, and she'd eat it if she liked it. If she didn't, she'd find something else. But she'd also been in third-world countries where people would eat anything to survive. Aidan didn't need to know about her philanthropic work. She tried to keep that low-key. Nico had put her in charge of the Lamon Foundation, the non-profit brand of the House of Lamon. She would not brag about that to Aidan.

"I like to cook," she did admit. "I enjoy the solitude and hominess of creating a meal and sitting at the table to enjoy it."

"You surprise me, Princess Fancy Pants."

Grimacing at that name, she went to the stove and took a deep breath, thinking he was full of surprises, too. "What is this concoction?"

"Taco soup."

"You and Annabelle love your tacos."

"We ate them a lot growing up."

Cara didn't push him to explain. Their mother Caron would never win Mother of the Year. She'd neglected her children and kept her husband drugged, all while she wooed Dallas society and tried to manhandle anyone who got in her way. Now, she sat in a minimum-security prison for the crimes she'd committed when she was in charge at Castle Department Store.

Trying to imagine her own mother in prison, Cara decided she could tolerate being with Aidan for a few hours. He'd probably be gone soon, anyway.

"You never did tell me why you're staying here," she said after he dipped her a bowl of the southwestern-style soup that consisted of shredded chicken, beans, chunks of tomato, and a spicy sauce. "Or which room you're staying in."

Dropping a few sprigs of fresh cilantro over her soup, he turned and dipped his, sat it on the long breakfast table, and then brought over sour cream, cheese, and a bag of corn chips.

"I'm finishing up the new security system that Johnny

and I are overseeing. Now that the Lone Star store is up and running, Johnny and my sister are back at Big Castle making goo-goo eyes at each other all the time. I need to tweak a few things with the security here, obviously."

"Obviously," she retorted with pride, "I managed to override a few things in the system."

"So I heard when the alarm went off." He sampled the soup before saying, "Beside some immediate problems," and he gave her a stern stare on that note, "since the new technology store is off I-20 and only about fifteen miles from the ranch, Nico suggested I crash here instead of driving through rush-hour traffic back to the Castle estate. He also wanted the ranch house secure since people will be arriving for the wedding. Johnny and I oversaw installing the security, and I'm still tweaking all the bells and whistles while Tobias is cleaning and making trips to town for supplies."

Tobias was the ranch foreman who'd been a fixture at the ranch for as long as she could remember. "Tobias's still around?"

"He's the boss."

"Well, it's nice to see you and my brother bonding."

"Are you being serious or sarcastic?"

"A little of both. He never wants me to come to the ranch alone. He thinks I'm still twelve."

"And he guards you like a hawk?"

"Like a big old bear. It's a bit stifling."

Aidan dipped his head, glancing over at her with that sexy-solemn twist of a smile. "You don't want me here."

He hadn't asked a question. He'd made it a statement. A

correct statement.

"Well, I was surprised to see you staring at me with those dark prince eyes."

"Well, I was surprised to find you on the couch in a wedding gown staring at me with those dove-gray eyes." Giving her a brooding look, he said, "What happened? Cold feet? Coming to your senses? Or … something else?"

Of all the men in the world, why did he have to be the one to see her humiliation? She couldn't tell him what had really happened. He'd nod his head and call her Princess Fancy Pants again, with smug satisfaction at that.

"I'd rather not talk about it." He still hadn't told her which room he had squatter's rights on. She hoped it wasn't the one across from hers upstairs. The images moving through her head would keep her awake every night.

He gave her another solemn stare. "You're hiding out."

"You're in my house."

"I told you I got here first."

"We have to remedy this. I suggest you find a hotel room. Or the barn has some cozy bunks."

"And I suggest you look outside."

After pushing back her chair and standing, she went to the big window and gasped. "Is that sleet?"

"Yes, and more on the way." He dropped some chips into his soup and dug in. "An icy winter storm is about to hit the state of Texas. We might get snowed in together, Princess Fancy Pants."

Cara groaned, returning to the table and plopping onto her chair. "This can't be happening."

"Mother Nature," he said with a shrug. "She has her moods."

He seemed to be referring to her with that stoic observation. Mad, she picked up her spoon and started eating.

She was hungry, and the soup tasted spicy and soothing.

"She eats." He grinned at her. "You're so thin, I wondered."

"Thin?" He'd said that without a trace of a compliment. "You don't like thin women?"

"I didn't say that," he replied, his eyes as black as the stormy night. Then his gaze moved to her lips.

Cara felt the burn of a blush moving down her neck. *Curses on you, Toby Keith.*

"What happened with you and your groom?"

"None of your business."

"How did you manage to pull off a near-wedding without Nico or your mother knowing?"

"None of your business."

"You do know that if you left a man standing at the altar, it will probably be all over social media—" he stopped and checked his watch, "—right about now."

"No," she said, the spicy soup congealing in her stomach. "No, no. I came here to be alone. I don't need you pointing out the drama of my life to me." Shrugging, she added, "He requested a secret wedding. He claimed to be related to the British Royals, and that we had to keep it private. He didn't need or want the publicity. Why would he announce it to the world now when he demanded secrecy then?"

"Your wording is telling. You said he *claimed to be* related to royalty. Did you doubt that?"

She hated Aidan's deliberate questions. "I began to doubt," she admitted, since she had no one else to confide in right now. "But … I really wanted him to be the real deal."

"And now you think he's not?"

"Yes. But … it's over. My lawyer confronted him, but he shoved him away and … disappeared out a side entrance. I don't think he'll bother me again."

"Why would your lawyer confront him?"

She squirmed. Hoping to keep this embarrassing incident contained, she did not want to blurt it all out to this man.

"To escort him away." Looking down, she added, "Awkward, but it's over."

"That *was* then, Cara. This *is* now. If you made him look bad, all bets for privacy are off. He'll want to retaliate. You've seen this before when people break up. All kinds of unpleasant things show up on the internet." He paused, letting her absorb that, and then added, "He could make life difficult. Especially since you're a Lamon … and a runaway bride of sorts. The gossip rags will love that angle."

"Right," she said, coming out of her fog and the numbness that had surrounded her since she'd gotten on that plane. "Trey could be the kind to turn the tables, I think. Things could get dicey. My lawyer will continue the investigation."

Even though he'd gotten away with a lot of foundation money and some of her personal funds, Trey wouldn't be too happy about her standing him up. Especially if he couldn't have the rest of the promised cash, which she would certainly never give him now.

Hoping her ex-fiancé would disappear and leave her alone, she couldn't bring herself to tell Aidan the whole truth. Trey had convinced her the funds she'd moved to a private bank would go toward the Wellington Corporation's non-profit orphanage in Africa. But Trey had convinced her to transfer part of it—to get things going. Right.

"Cara, what are you not telling me?"

"What I'm *not* telling you—this is really none of your business," she retorted, her heart still too bruised to talk about this. But Aidan had that quiet way of drawing things out of her. Things like her heart, her lips, her need to find someone she could trust. Could she trust him?

He patiently waited.

She let out a sigh. "I can't be sure how many other people knew about the wedding. We had handlers helping us, but … I left the church in a rush after I told my lawyer to explain things to Trey." Looking around, she said, "I don't even know where my phone is. Or my luggage for that matter."

"I found both on the back porch near the security box you managed to mangle."

Feeling sheepish, she said, "This could be bad. So bad."

"I can scrub some things for you."

"I took my own shower, thank you."

His gaze locked on her lips again. "I mean social media and press wise. Make it all go away."

That got her attention. "Really?"

He sat back, folding his arms over his chest. "Really. But only if you don't send me out into the cold." Then he leaned in and said, "Take it from someone who's still reeling from one of the biggest scandals in Texas. The press can be brutal, and social media can latch onto something this juicy and turn it into an unsubstantiated nightmare. We'd have reporters camped out here, at the estate, and at the store, like when the news broke about my mother."

"I can't let that happen. Nico and Eleanor deserve a beautiful wedding, but this could cause major problems. But I can't stay here with you either."

"Relax. I usually fall asleep on the couch in the office, get a quick shower, and leave as the sun is coming up to head to the build site. I won't bother you at all."

When she didn't respond, he shrugged. "If you think you can handle this on your own, I'll sleep in the bunkhouse. But I could be doing damage control for you in a matter of minutes, and ... it's much warmer in here. Or at least, it was."

She glared. Fumed. She weighed her choices. Trey could be trying to get to her money right this minute.

Finally, she sighed. "Let me finish my soup."

Chapter Three

AIDAN FORGOT ABOUT sleep, getting straight to work finding out the truth about Cara Lamon. He needed to know what was really going on. He'd turned a blind eye to his mother's crimes and he regretted that, so he had no intention of protecting another woman who might be up to no good. Cara's cryptic answers and secretive wedding set off alarms. He needed answers. His mother's betrayal had rocked his world, and it had made him distrustful.

He also regretted how he'd mostly ignored Papa Castle's attempts to be a real father to Annabelle and him. But he'd worked hard now for redemption by overseeing the building of the innovative new technology store. He could not afford another corporate espionage scandal, especially since the new store would open early next year. He'd use his wicked talents for good instead of evil and get to the bottom of this new scandal—before it blew up in Cara's face.

Why did she have to show up here now, when he needed the quiet and the solitude? Thinking about that pair of shoes she'd left by the sofa, he remembered moving them to the staircase. Shoes had gotten this whole crazy year started. It was always about the shoes with women.

Aidan had to admit, he'd emerged out of his self-protective cocoon lately. And Cara Lamon had been one of the reasons for that. She knew shoes in the same way Audrey Hepburn knew Tiffany's. Through and through. Now he wanted to know her, through and through.

She'd certainly broadened his boring horizons. Their one brief encounter at the ball had left an impression.

For as long as he could remember, he'd operated on his own. Bored as a kid, he'd played video games, but he'd also learned how video games were created. He'd spent a lot of time online, teaching himself how to write code and create or find anything he wanted in the virtual world. Then after acing his ATC and all the other required tests, he'd applied and gotten accepted to the University of Texas and later, MIT—the Massachusetts Institute of Technology.

In high school, he'd been a sullen nerd. A geek of the worst kind. The boys tried to bully him, while the girls flirted with him, but only to watch him shy away and blush.

He didn't like those types of games.

His brain had always been better than his brawn but after a near run-in at a bar with a big football player, his college roommates had taken him to the gym. He'd also become appreciative of being physically able to take care of himself.

Now, however, he quaked in his boots because a petite dynamo wearing a wedding gown had come home to hide away from the world. How was he supposed to find the solitude he always needed when the scent of her exotic perfume followed him around this big, sprawling house?

"Have you done it?" she asked, two coffee mugs in her hands as she slid into the office and stood staring at him.

Glancing up from the humongous desk by the window, he shook his head. "Patience, my pretty. These things take time."

She handed Aidan his coffee. "I got in touch with my lawyer." Holding her own mug close, she stared at the brew. "He's put his investigator on trailing Trey because, like you, he's concerned Trey might try something else."

"It makes sense," Aidan replied. "But I'm going to try to head him off at the pass."

Cara went to the window and checked outside. "That's not sleet anymore. It's snowing."

Aidan stood, holding his mug, and gazed out into the gray-washed back yard. The security light showed the fat, shining white drops floating down in a heavy veil of lacy snow. "Stranded."

"You can say that again. Texas is not used to dealing with a lot of the white stuff, and we know the ice will make it worse." She waved her hand at the laptop. "Well, we've got nothing better to do, so let's get at it."

Aidan could think of a lot of better things to do, but no. He didn't need to go there. Cara Lamon was so out of his league it wasn't even a daydream. It would be a nightmare.

She glowed in the spotlight.

He shunned the spotlight.

He hid his flaws well enough, but he'd do whatever it took to protect Castle's. That meant he'd be investigating the woman who made his hard heart beat faster.

"Well, we have a lot of work ahead of us," he said, thinking he'd do her this big favor if she'd leave him alone.

Besides, he was curious and interested enough to want to crack this case.

"Such as?" she asked, dragging him back to the moment.

Her big eyes had been the first thing about her that had distracted him. Her lips, the second. And that trace of an Italian accent didn't hurt either.

He didn't really want to go any further than that.

"We need to delete all of your online activity that might involve your fiancé. Websites, data, and social media sites, as well as photos, personal information that might be on the web, old searches, maybe even email accounts."

"Mine I can do, but how do we get into Trey's accounts? He does not have a huge social media footprint."

"Give me as much information on him as you can, and I'll do the rest. I'll save it all on a thumb-drive, so you'll at least have a record of this. Better left unexplained."

"Oh." Then those stormy eyes widened again. "Oh. Right."

"Do you plan to press charges?"

Surprise blossomed on her face, and then she started fidgeting. "I'd press charges, yes. But … I'm not sure I'd get very far unless I catch him red-handed with the money." Shrugging, she added, "And I can't really charge him for not signing a prenup."

Aidan sat up straight. "Is that what this is about? The man wouldn't sign a prenup?"

Pressing her teeth against her bottom lip, she cast her eyes away. "That's part of it, yes. But I also don't want him to get access to the rest of the funds I thought he'd be using for his charity."

"Again, are you planning to press charges?"

"How can I when it will be hard to prove any of this?"

"It might be hard, but we can try. If he's running a con, law enforcement might not want to get involved. Like going down a rabbit hole because a lot of con victims are too humiliated to come forward."

"Well, I *am* humiliated," she admitted, her face twisting into defeat and regret. "That's why I wanted to let him go."

"Why not be your usual smart, demanding self?" Aidan asked, wanting that tough façade back. "I'd think you'd send out a militia to stop this man from hurting innocent people."

"You're right," she said, putting down her coffee cup. "If a friend came to me with this ridiculous story, I'd force her to head straight to the authorities. I was so in shock, so confused, that I took the coward's path. I ran away."

"But you ran here. Home. The best place to be now as it turns out."

"Because you're here?" She paced and huffed. "I could do worse, I suppose."

"I'll take that as a vote of confidence."

She nodded, her features hidden in shadows. "So where do we start? I'm sure he's hiding in one of those rabbit holes right now, but I don't think he was a con man. I do believe he liked my money, a lot, though."

"So the goal is to save face and keep this from the press, especially before your brother's wedding."

"Yes."

"We'll delete your shopping habits, so no one can trace

you buying a wedding gown or plane tickets or booking a venue. Anything that can show you were about to marry a man in secret."

"He claimed his people booked the venue. He also bought the plane tickets. But the dress came off the sample rack from the House of Lamon."

"But … someone had to bring it to you off the rack, right?"

"The staff is very discreet. I told them I needed it for a friend. And I paid them cash."

"Smart, but still … more cash can loosen sealed lips."

"Okay, all right. Do it."

"You'll need to deactivate your social networking accounts for a while. As I said, probably your email accounts, too. No phone calls either."

"I can't do that. I have business to attend to. I'll need to keep my official accounts open."

"Okay, limit your calls and web browsing and use the land line as much as possible. What kind of business—and don't say none of my business."

She hesitated, sighed, and fidgeted with her hair. "Believe it or not, I do have a job within the House of Lamon."

"Really?"

"Don't look so surprised. Our mother taught us to work hard and carry our own weight even if we've both failed miserably at times."

"So what do you do?"

"You want to know? All right then. I'm in charge of the Lamon Foundation. I pick and choose which charities we will support, and I decide how much money we'll donate. I travel all over the world to make sure our money is being put to good use, and because I like getting involved in a personal way."

Shocked, Aidan held up a hand. "Wait, what?"

She shrugged at his surprise. "I'm a people person and I'm good with organizing events, so my mother handpicked me for philanthropic duties."

"I'm trying to wrap my brain around this," he said, his honesty sounding brutal even to him. "I thought—"

"I know what you think," she replied, clearly flustered. "I don't talk about it much. Mother also taught us to be discreet and low-key and no, I haven't been that in my personal life, but I do adhere to that rule regarding my work. Mother said do good, be good, but don't go around shouting your good deeds to the world. Because the world will scoff and think you're out to get something in return."

"She's right there," Aidan said, impressed and wishing he'd had a mother like that. His mother had shouted her great deeds while she carried on with criminals. He sure hoped Cara wasn't doing the same with him. Did Nico know something he'd never shared about his sister?

"It's been hard, hasn't it?" She looked at the fire, but he thought he saw empathy in her eyes. "Do you miss your mother?"

"Yes, like a sore tooth," he retorted. "She's my mother, so I try to call her and visit her when I can. She's mad at all of us. But even if she gets out in five years, she's not allowed on the estate property or in Castle Department Store again."

"What will she do?"

"Probably settle down in a modest house, find a job at a lesser department store, and be glad she didn't do worse."

"Is that why *you're* hiding out here?" Cara asked, her voice quiet. "Because you're still trying to get out from under her dark shadow?"

"I'm not hiding out. I like my privacy."

He didn't want to discuss his own pain.

She didn't press him on it. "As do I, so let's get my online footprint cleaned up."

Cara seemed sincere, but he had trust issues with women. Most didn't get his need to be alone and away from the crowds. He wouldn't admit he might be hiding out, too. He'd had enough of the roar of press conferences and the shouting headlines from newspapers and tabloids.

Not even noticing his doubt, Cara went on. "I've tried to do my work and help people who are in need in a quiet, unassuming way. I had planned on doing that in Bali with my new husband, but … that didn't go so well."

Aidan began to see the truth here. "Did this Trey person know about your low-key good works?"

"I told him when we got serious. I wanted him to understand I'd be traveling a lot for my work, and I wouldn't stop after we were married."

"I take it he knew you'd be handling millions of dollars in charity funding?"

"Yes." She grew quiet, a mask moving over her face. "Yes, he did." Twirling a silky strand of hair in one hand while she sipped coffee, she added, "He liked being low-key, too. Rarely let anyone photograph him."

Whirling, she shook her head, her eyes going wide. "Which makes perfect sense now, of course. He truly did only want the money, not me." Lowering her head, she said, "You must see me as a silly socialite, too dumb to see what was in front of her face."

"I see a woman who trusted her heart to a man who has no heart."

Aidan put down his coffee cup, giving her his attention. "Did your so-called-groom tell you about a cause he had, a cause he wanted the Lamon Foundation to invest in? And if he did mention such a cause, I'm sure he was completely convincing and charming. So charming he touched all of your emotions?"

She moved to the window, stared out into the snowy night. "Possibly."

"Just tell me, yes or no."

Finally she turned, her eyes full of agony. "Yes. Yes. Yes. He reeled me in, asking me a lot of questions, comparing how we'd both come from broken homes, his being from royalty. That's why he wanted privacy, he said. And I told him I liked to stay low-key for that very same reason. I told him about how things were changing so quickly in my life. Good things, but still very stressful. He was so empathetic, so real. He said he did philanthropic work, too, to ease his conscience for being so blessed, so rich."

Pushing at her hair, she finally looked up at Aidan. "He took a big check after we were engaged—a loan until he could get his finances transferred. My lawyers and accountants got suspicious and suggested a prenup. Trey refused to sign one. That and other concerns forced me to walk away from the wedding."

"How much did you give him?" Aidan asked, his hands curling into fists.

"Enough that if I tell my brother, Nico will probably kill him."

"Not if I get to him first," Aidan replied.

CARA'S HEART DID a nervous flip. She believed this man. The sheer anger in his dark eyes made her step back. "You don't need to get involved in this."

He glanced around. "I'm here and I became involved the minute I found you on the couch."

"Then I'll leave."

He waved his hand toward the window. "Not tonight, you won't. If you don't let me help you get ahead of this, your brother will hear about it from your lawyer or worse, he'll see it in the headlines. We need to catch a thief. And soon."

Closing her eyes, she could guess what the press would say. "I run a clean operation, and all the money goes straight to those we're trying to help. But some of the money is sitting in a bank and … Trey has access to it, but I have to be with him in order for him to do anything with it."

"What do you mean?"

"He has foundation money … and about one-hundred-

31

thousand dollars from my trust fund."

Aidan leaned back in the leather desk chair. "He scammed you, and then he wanted to marry you to get his hands on more Lamon dollars."

"It appears that way, yes."

"How fail-proof did you make this bank deposit?"

"I always use iris or fingerprint scans to get access to foundation money. But … because we were getting married and traveling so soon, we were supposed to transfer the money before we went to Bali."

Aidan gave her a look that told her everything. She'd been the worst kind of gullible. A lonely, needy woman who pretended she had it all together.

"You need to go to Nico and tell him the truth."

"No, not before the wedding. I won't ruin things for him and Eleanor." Lowering her head, she said, "I tend to date too quickly and then break things off. It's a pattern, and my overbearing brother is tired of it. I stopped sharing my love life with him for that reason."

"Then why did you decide to get married two weeks before their wedding? Were you going to bring your new groom as your plus-one and spring him on them?"

"He had business to attend immediately after our wedding," she said on a weak note. "I planned to come here by myself after we'd had a few days together in Bali. Afterward, I planned to return with Trey and announce our wedding after the holidays."

Aidan stared down at his laptop, tapping the keys. "I can only imagine what business he had planned. Your Trey has all the markings of a real psychopath."

"He seemed so wonderfully normal and … royal."

Aidan shot her an ounce of pity and then got serious, his mind apparently on finding data. "That's how these types operate. He has no qualms about what he's doing. He can mimic anyone to blend in. He'll pretend to care, and he'll act like a decent human being. He'll promise you the world. But once he has what he wants, he moves on."

She glared at Aidan, wanting to hate him for how he'd summed things up. "He also preferred having intimate dinners at home rather than going out. He rarely went to events with me and when he did, we had to be careful that we only looked like friends. Nothing more. He didn't like having his picture taken."

"Perfect. He really knows his stuff regarding rich social-ites, doesn't he? I'm thinking he planned some of these intimate, romantic dinners at quaint, out-of-the-way restaurants and country inns, quiet chateaus, or secluded beach houses?"

Cara let out a sigh that caught and held, more like a sob, the reality settling over her with a cold that left her shivering. "That sounds exactly like Trey."

It hurt to accept he didn't love her, but only wanted to use the Lamon name and the security of having her money in some faraway bank. Not a prince, not royal, and not rich, but a cad and a horrible, cruel person.

"I can't believe I've been duped." She slanted her head to the left, trying to work the kinks out of her neck. "And to think with all the others, I handled breaking up discreetly.

But … I didn't care about them the way I did about Trey."

Aidan's dark gaze slid over her. "Trey picked the wrong princess to mess with."

Sinking down on the chair across from the desk, she studied him. "Why do you care?"

Giving her an eyebrow lift, he said, "My family has been dealing with this kind of stuff all year long. Things are beginning to settle down. Castle's doesn't need another dust-up."

A heated blush made Cara sweat underneath her sweater. "I'm sorry. I didn't consider what you and Annabelle have been through. You've both dealt with a lot lately, and so has Eleanor. But I don't need to involve you. I'll figure this out."

"I'm involved," he said, shaking his head. "Do you think I'd walk away after what this man has done to you?" He wagged a finger at her. "You really should press charges."

"You *are* concerned." That touched her even in her mortified state of mind. "Thank you, Aidan."

Pounding the keys, he said, "Don't thank me yet. I'll try to get ahead of this, but there is the matter of the money. Trey will want to move the rest of it pretty quickly. You say he can't do that without you. So what exactly does that mean?"

"I have to be there with him. As I said, the bank officer demands an iris scan. Both Trey's and mine. That's how I set it up."

"And Trey had to agree. You'd get married, and he'd be able to get to the money once you were his wife."

"Yes. I set it up that way per the advice of my lawyer and

accountant. Now I understand why they insisted. I'm such an idiot." Shrugging, she said, "That explains why he seemed so tense the day we went to the bank together."

Aidan didn't dispute that. "I'll do what I can, but this seems to run deeper than you realize. Besides, I like Nico, I love my sister Eleanor, and I guess I kind of like you, too. This could ruin their wedding or at least distract from their joy."

"Distract their joy?" She stood and put her hands on her hips, disappointment dragging her down. "Well, I'd never want to do that. I've said as much." Then she narrowed her eyes. "And I so appreciate how you might *kind of* like me."

She wanted to ask him if he'd 'kind of' liked her when he'd kissed her senseless.

He stopped typing, stared into her eyes, and then moved his gaze over her lips. "I barely know you, but I'd like to get to know you better."

The way he said that in a low, husky way made her heart burn with a white-hot heat. Why did she get the jitters around a man who wasn't her type? Could it be that she got all antsy with Aidan *because* he *wasn't* her type?

"I've messed things up with everyone," she said, her tone dejected. "I wasn't thinking clearly, obviously."

"Then why did you agree to this lamebrain wedding?"

"I was in love," she shouted, her heart shattering, tears clogging her throat. "Trey Wellington is a charming, gorgeous Englishman who convinced me he was related to the queen herself. He gave me an antique yellow diamond engagement ring. I left it behind."

"And why does that matter so much?"

"It wasn't about that," she said, knowing she sounded shallow. "I fell for him. Everything about him. The whole package, the kind of Prince Charming women dream about."

Not like the dark knight sitting here giving her that moody eye.

"And you fell for him without verifying?"

"I did verify. I had him thoroughly checked— background, lineage, and anything I could find. It all checked out. I'm not quite as stupid as you seem to think. I've been down this road before with men interested in Lamon money, but no one has ever scammed me. I thought this time things were right."

Aidan stood, too, his hands in his jeans pockets. "So why did you bother to show up for the wedding if you decided not to go through with it?"

Because I thought I could make him tell me the truth.

She really didn't want to explain this, but Aidan had her cornered and he knew it. "My lawyer and my investigator kept at it up until the day of the wedding. Because I wanted to give him this extreme amount of money for his *noble* cause, and I'd already moved some of the funds."

"What kind of noble cause?" Aidan asked, his gaze going soft.

"An orphanage in Africa," she admitted. "He threw out a lot of names, then showed me pages and pages of legitimate-looking paperwork."

"An orphanage." Aidan started up hitting the keys again. "That would tug at your heartstrings."

"It did. The pictures he showed me broke my heart."

"And the whole time, he planned a secret wedding at an undisclosed location. A wedding I'm guessing he rushed you into because he loved you, and he couldn't wait to be with you."

She cringed. How could he work and insult her at the same time? "Well, when you say it like that, it really stings."

"I'm sorry but if you want this fixed, you have to be completely honest with me."

"I'm trying to be honest, but I'm not quite ready to spill all the personal details of my affair to you."

"Did he rush you, get you all worked up, promise you the moon and the stars?"

"Yes, he did rush the wedding," she admitted. "And I didn't care. I was in love for the first time. He had me snowed over. Now, ironically, I'm snowed in with the one other man in the world I'd rather not be with."

"Well, when you say it like that, it sure does sting," he mimicked, barely glancing up. "I'm sorry I'm *that* man. The one other one, I mean. I don't want or need your money, but I do want to help you. I mean, somebody needs to help you out of this mess. Luckily for you, I'm good at this kind of stuff."

"Does it require you doing anything illegal?"

"Did you and Prince Trey do anything illegal?"

"I didn't," she said. "At least, I'm not aware of anything."

She'd acted out during her teen years and done some things she'd had to hide, but … that had nothing to do with this. Her motives had been pure, even if her tactics had been misguided.

Cara thought about telling Aidan, but she changed her mind.

He didn't need to hear about her troubled youth days. Not yet, anyway.

"I have work to do," he replied, his tone grim. "With a man like that, you don't know what he had you sign or who he has behind him. We have to protect you and your interests."

"What's your plan?"

"I'm going to create a fake online presence. An obscure social media profile that can be our entry into exposing your Trey."

"Exposing? I never agreed to that."

"It's the only way to catch him," Aidan replied. "You won't be involved. It will be anonymous, and I can make it look like any number of people he might have conned. He won't know who's outing him until it's too late."

"That sounds dangerous."

"Only if you don't know what you're doing. But I know this stuff. I help write code for people all the time. I can hack into any account, and no one will ever know."

"You'll draw him out and … possibly get the money back?"

"I don't know about the money yet. If he's good, he'll hide what he has right away in an untraceable offshore account. He won't leave any footprints, but I'll find him."

This Aidan scared her almost as much as losing money to a con artist did. But he was her only hope. "We don't have much time."

"No, we don't. I'm going to get things started. People like your Trey hate the web. It's like a spider web to them. They don't want to be trapped or drawn in, so they tend to avoid it. As you said, no photos, no public appearances together. That way, it's your word against his."

"You'll be careful?"

"I'm always careful."

She nodded, holding her tongue while he went back to his laptop. Now Aidan had her wondering if Trey had done anything else illegal under her name and reputation.

"How did your lawyer find you in time to stop things?"

"I told him where I'd be," she said. "If something happened to someone I loved, I'd want to know. Or if something happened to me, they'd need to know." *In case I panicked and changed my mind.*

"Good move."

"Thank you."

"You got cold feet, and left him at the altar?"

"Yes. I called Trey into the bridal room to see how he'd react about a prenup." She swallowed back tears. "I'd hoped he'd declare his undying love for me and sign the papers."

"But he didn't?"

"No." She put her head in her hands. "He declared his love while making me feel horrible for doubting him." Lifting her chin, she spilled the worst of it. "He said we'd need to get to that money soon. His foundation counted on such donations. Why would I insist on a prenup when we were going to do good things together? After that, I couldn't do it. I couldn't go through with it. I kissed him—a goodbye kiss, but he didn't have a clue."

"Did anyone question him regarding the money?"

"No. I left since I knew he couldn't get to the rest of it without me. I'd lost the money he already had, so I told my lawyer to handle things. Trey managed to slip away when they were in discussions."

Aidan rubbed his five o'clock shadow. "Hmm. That could work in your favor."

"How so?"

"He's counting on you not wanting any publicity since these types of things are humiliating, so he'll probably move on to the next mark. We could turn the tables on him. I assume you had the money secured."

"My people are on that, yes. But they're being very discreet. He is not to get near the rest of the money without me."

"If we put out the word regarding his shenanigans, but don't mention your name—"

"Then we might be able to clear this up within a matter of days?"

"Possibly. But we have to be quick. He'll run for the border. Probably go to ground until things cool down. Then he'll start all over again, with a new identity, and move on."

"We can't let him do that. No one should have to go through this."

She couldn't believe this had happened, but having Aidan here helped. If he hadn't been so determined, she would have probably slept right through the snowstorm outside and the firestorm in her own life, then spent the next week or so pouting while her tragic debacle could have been plastered all over the internet. What had she been thinking?

She'd never trust a man again. Never.

But right now, she had to trust this man with her life and her reputation and her family's legacy. Brilliant with devices and technology, he'd also had first-hand experience with this kind of thing. She didn't have any other choice.

"Can you really do this, Aidan?"

"Just watch me, Princess Fancy Pants," he replied, those dark eyes making shivers shimmy down her spine.

"Oh, I'll be watching," she said. "I'm going to watch and learn and I'm never going to let a con man get the best of me again."

Chapter Four

AIDAN HAD WORKED late into the night to erase a lot of data on Cara that might make its way to the top of social media sites. But Trey Wellington had been very thorough in making sure he hadn't left a heavy online footprint. Aidan had managed to work around that, creating a flash drive with the details he scraped up. Then he'd set up the fake account, and planned to add to it after he had some facts on Trey Wellington. But he still had concerns regarding Cara's part in this. She had indicated she'd been thorough in protecting the money, but a good con man could make the impossible happen and set it up to look like her fault.

He'd told Cara before she went up to bed last night that he planned to start a file on Trey Wellington. The charismatic con artist had the misfortune of messing with a Lamon. And now, a Castle.

Aidan had taken a personal interest in bringing this man to justice. But to do that, he needed evidence.

But he needed to understand Cara, too. She wanted it over and done before her brother found out. She'd used thousands of dollars of foundation funding to fuel the bogus charity Trey had managed to create. That put her in a bad spot. It could jeopardize her charitable work.

She also had money from her trust fund, which was legally hers to do what she wanted with, of course. She'd spent a good amount of that while gallivanting with Wellington. But to save face, she needed this gone. She didn't want to disappoint her family or become a laughingstock all over the globe.

Now that he knew she had cold feet about making a commitment and he'd found some brief news articles to back that up, he could at least understand why Trey's trickery had hurt her to the core.

But she could still be hiding something. He intended to dig deep into her business affairs, too. He'd called a friend to help him gather more information on both her and Trey.

Sooner or later, Cara could have some explaining to do.

But not if Aidan could find Wellington first, and not if he kept his findings to himself until he had proof.

He didn't want to doubt her, but … how could he trust her at this point?

Lost in his thoughts, Aidan glanced up when he heard voices in the kitchen. Who else had come to visit? He hadn't heard a vehicle since the snow and ice had accumulated and stayed. Impossible for Texans to drive in these conditions.

He stood, stretched his tired muscles, and then checked the clock. Six-thirty AM. He'd slept on the couch about three hours after staying up to around two in the morning. He'd planned to go to the worksite today, but the foreman called and told him they wouldn't be working anyway. More snow and ice on the way, and his men lived out from the city. Most of the major thoroughfares were closed, trees were down on power lines, and the roads were a treacherous mess. A winter-storm watch covered half the state.

A bad delay, but Aidan could still do some work from the office here—talking to vendors, processing orders, and going over blueprints again.

He'd done all he could do for Cara for now, since he had to be careful not to bring his one-man vendetta to the attention of the NSA, the cyber-crimes unit, or the FBI. Not to mention Interpol. But exposing an international con man couldn't be all bad if Aidan kept things anonymous.

So he strolled to the kitchen to find breakfast, check on their guest, and to see how Cara had slept.

"Look who I found!" With a warning grin, she waved her arm toward the scrawny man sitting at the table, a plate of fried eggs and crisp bacon in front of him.

He should have known.

Aidan went to the coffee pot, playing along with her pretend happiness. "Tobias, how are you?"

The aged caretaker let out a ragged chuckle. "Finer than frog hair. And even better after seeing this vision at the door this morning. She's a tad prettier than you."

"Thanks," Aidan said, laughing as he looked over at Cara. Tobias often stopped in for breakfast. "And I have to agree with you on that."

She wore a loose sweater, leggings, and fuzzy-topped boots. Her hair fell in soft layers to her shoulders and her lips looked good, even without lipstick.

Her eyes held a dare that made him want to laugh while he walked away. Because he should walk away. He didn't need this beautiful distraction while he did his level best to make the technology store one of the finest in the Metroplex, maybe even all of Texas. Just like his sister Annabelle, Aidan needed to prove himself to the world. Especially the Castle world. With a mother in jail and no father to speak of, he was on his own. Alone.

He'd liked it that way until he'd kissed her. And he resented her for that—and for this brilliant interruption of his solitude. Annabelle had always teased him about being the absentminded professor, never noticing anything or anyone around him, but he had sure noticed Cara Lamon.

To counter his raw feelings, he said, "Tobias, did you hear the alarm going off last night?"

Tobias, all wiry beard and even more wiry hair, glanced up with a clueless, openmouthed expression. "Huh?"

"Tobias's cabin is a bit back from this house," Cara said in his defense. "And it was late when I arrived, not to mention the weather."

"And I'm half-deaf," Tobias added, his hearing seemingly intact right now.

He must have come with the ranch since he'd been here since forever, according to Nico. Tobias acted as foreman and stayed year-round while other employees came and went. Everyone came to him for advice and help. Aidan wondered if he had any relation to Claude from the main Castle store or Saul from the new Lone Star store. He sure reminded Aidan of them.

Turning to Cara, Aidan asked, "Why didn't you wake Tobias last night, anyway?"

She shrugged, rearranged all that gorgeous hair. "I was cold and wearing a wedding gown. Besides, after the driver dropped me off, I sat by the pool and finished off the champagne until I got really cold. I'm not sure I could have made it to Tobias's place in the dark and with sleet beginning to form."

And in her slightly tipsy state, Aidan remembered.

Tobias chewed on his bacon and nodded. "Not to mention, I'da had a heart attack for sure, seeing a beautiful young bride at my door. I mean, I've been married four times. Don't want to do that again." Then he gave Cara a sincere glance. "Ain't none of my business, beyond that."

"I shared my plight with you, but you shall not repeat any of this to my family. Right, Tobias?"

The old man gave her a lopsided grin. "I don't even remember what we were talking about."

Aidan took in the scenario. Cara and Tobias seemed chummy, but she obviously hadn't told the man why she'd left her groom. Yet, Tobias appeared satisfied with her explanation. "So you heard nothing, and Cara did nothing? Except set off the alarm that you also didn't hear."

"That about sums it up, son," Tobias replied. "I keep to myself after hours, and I sleep like an old log."

"Because you take care of this place," Cara said with a glare toward Aidan. "We've never needed a fancy alarm system before."

Tobias wagged a finger at her. "Times have changed. The Lamons are true Texas royalty now that y'all hooked up with Castle Department Store."

"I guess we are more exposed," she said, her eyes losing some of their luster. "We don't want to be hassled or taken advantage of."

"Nope. And I ain't as good as I once was," Tobias admitted with a shake of humility. "Used to could fight off three, four men at a time." Winking at Cara, he added, "Now I'm down to one, maybe two."

Aidan snorted at that. "No need to fight off anyone. Once the security system is finished, this place will be like Fort Knox."

Tobias snorted back. "Then I can sleep even better." Going on, he asked Cara, "So are you here for the big to-do coming up the week before Christmas?"

"What to-do?" she quipped, that darkness still in her eyes.

But she handed Aidan a plate of eggs and bacon, her haughty expression bordering on disdain.

"You always did have a smart sense of humor," Tobias said, his coffee cup held with two hands. "That wedding is gonna be something else."

"Are you coming?" Cara asked the old man, hope in her words.

"Wouldn't miss it for the world," Tobias said, his eyes misty. "I love Miss Lila like my own, and I love you and Nico like that, too. Good to see your brother settling down." He gave her a stretched-eye grin. "And now that you arrived in a wedding dress, when is some lucky man gonna snag you up?"

Cara's gaze hit Aidan's and held. "Never," she said with a

firm determination, her nose in the air. "I've decided marriage isn't for me."

Tobias stared at her while she eyed Aidan. Aidan remained calm, not making any sudden moves.

Tobias snorted again. "Suga', seeing as you showed up in a marriage dress, you might have left one standing … and that's your business. But real love sneaks up on you when you least expect it. Might want to keep the dress."

"You got that right about love sneaking up on people," she said before turning toward the stove, her head down. "I won't need the dress again, I can assure you."

Tobias squinted at Aidan, cutting his eyes between him and Cara before grinning. "If I were a betting man…"

After Tobias left, Aidan moved over to where Cara now stood staring out at the pastures and trees beyond the main yard. "Is that true, what you said to Tobias?"

"You mean regarding the alarm?"

"You know what I'm talking about," he replied. "Now you're against marriage? You'll let one stupid con man ruin you like that?"

"I'll never be that naïve again," she said, turning to walk away. "I won't let anyone take advantage of me again either, no matter how charming he is."

"Good thing I'm not charming," Aidan countered, just to test her.

"Good thing I'm not interested," she retorted before heading for the stairs.

"Ouch."

Aidan hurried to get dressed. He needed to check the

security system once again to find out what had gone wrong last night. Putting on a warm coat and a dark wool cap, he went outside to see what kind of damage Cara had done to his state-of-the-art system.

The answer lay on a table near the back door. She'd obviously tried her key. When that hadn't worked, she'd tried to either guess the password to the lock box or she'd tried to disarm it. The hammer lying on the table near the door had to be her weapon of choice since the lockbox was mangled and bent.

"Nice work, Princess Fancy Pants. That'll cost a pretty penny."

But then, she had a lot of pretty pennies to spare, didn't she? If he didn't count the ones she'd inadvertently given to Trey Wellington.

"SO WHAT'S *YOUR* plan?" Aidan asked Cara later that afternoon.

The fire crackled and hissed in the big den next to the office, but outside the snow continued to fall in soft fat flakes. All the rural areas and parts of the city were without power.

"What do you mean?" She'd cleaned the house, organized the pantry, taken notes for groceries, and found enough food to make lasagna for dinner. She enjoyed baking and cooking. And nesting was her way of coping with her troubles.

"You left your groom at the altar and came straight here," Aidan said after stoking the fire again. "Did you mean to stay hidden until the wedding? Or had you planned to go into town and face your brother?"

"My brother is still out of town," she reminded him. "Which is why I thought I'd be safe here." After sitting quietly for a moment, she tossed her hair. "I needed a quiet, secluded place to regain my equilibrium."

But finding him here had only made her even more confused. And disoriented. And now she was worried Trey would try to retaliate for her leaving him at the altar. Her brother's wedding had been publicized in several magazines, news reports, and social sites.

Trey wouldn't dare bother her here, but he could do something to get even. Something that could pop up at any time. Or at the worst time. Especially if Aidan's idea worked too well and brought Trey out of hiding.

"Do you ever plan to tell Nico what happened?"

"I told you not until after the wedding. I had *planned* to pull myself together over the next few days, call him, and tell him I'd be here waiting for our mother to arrive a few days before the wedding."

"Are you going to tell her the truth?"

"Eventually, everyone will know."

"But your goal is to keep this quite until after the big event?"

"That's what I've told you. Why are you still grilling me?"

He pointed out the window. "We're stranded, the

weather isn't letting up, and … your secret could blow wide open unless we can continue to contain it. Nico is somewhere in another part of the world. All the Castle stores are in good hands. The wedding is all planned, and a lot of people will start arriving here and at the estate for the big day. We're in a race with the clock to make sure you aren't exposed until you want to be exposed. If ever."

"Yes, and you said you had that under control."

"I do." He studied the laptop he'd placed on the coffee table. "But … in the meantime, we can work together to expose Trey Wellington, too."

"Without even leaving the house?"

"Of course. Without him even knowing we did it, just as I told you."

"How do I know I can trust *you*?" she asked, her heart pounding a warning. "What if this does blow up in my face?"

"We'll deal with it together," he said. "I won't let anything happen to you."

That had to be the nicest thing he'd ever said to her, even though they hadn't really talked that much.

But she wasn't buying it. "You can't make that promise."

"No, but I'll do my best to help you."

"Because of your loyalty to my brother and your sister?"

"That and … my loyalty to you." Leaning over, he smiled. "We're practically family in a weird way, so you have no choice. You have to trust me."

Cara didn't like that conclusion.

"I hope I won't live to regret this," she said.

But right now, here with him, she felt safe, cozy, and protected. Which made her trust him even less.

"My life is in your hands," she said. "Don't let me down."

Chapter Five

"YOU'RE A GOOD cook."

Cara turned from the stove toward Aidan with a small smile. "Thank you, I think. You said that with such disbelief, I can't believe it myself."

Feeling sheepish, he said, "You always seem to doubt my compliments."

"That's because you always frame them in that condescendingly surprised way."

"You're a good cook, Princess Fancy Pants. How's that?"

With a roll of her eyes, she went about loading the dishwasher. "Ever so much better."

"I guess I don't get it," he said as he brought his plate over. "Lasagna."

"I'm half Italian. What's not to get?"

"You being so domestic. I figured you had servants at your beck and call."

"We do but as I've told you, our mother taught us to be self-sufficient in all areas of our lives."

Aidan wondered if their mother had neglected to teach Cara about love or trusting con men. His own mother hadn't bothered much with explaining the details of life, so he and Annabelle had figured things out on their own. Now Annabelle was in love with Johnny. The head of visual merchandising engaged to the head of security. His sister, the ham, loved to shock people, but she'd finally found an audience of one. Johnny—easygoing and funny, but also quiet and reclusive. He centered Annabelle.

Another match made in Castle Land.

Aidan's mind went back to the night of the costume ball and how he'd kissed Cara in a secluded alcove somewhere between the shoe department and houseware and furnishings. Not a match, just a weak moment and some good champagne. He had to let it go. He'd accepted a lot of new changes over the last few months. His mother going to jail, his long-lost stepsister showing up, taking over control of Castle's, and getting engaged to Nico Lamon, as well as his sister finally maturing and settling down with Johnny, of all people. Things were changing around here, and Aidan had to keep up. He loved changing technology, but changing personal stuff? Not so much.

Too much to absorb and a year he'd never get over.

But … he'd had some good moments, too. Eleanor saw his talents in technology and had given him the opportunity he'd always dreamed of—opening a technology mecca with the Castle name behind it. Everything had been moving along.

Until this interesting beauty had showed up in a wedding dress.

So he talked business, which had always been his go-to topic when he needed to work through something. "Well, while you were putting together this amazing lasagna, I worked on shredding your online history. At least for the last six months."

"That's the time I spent with Trey."

"Yes. Deleting things off any technology device doesn't mean it's gone forever. But internal shredding and erasing can help in that area."

"I'm glad I packed all of my devices then. They all need a deep cleaning."

"To be safe," he added. "You can rebuild your sites, and I did save some of it on an external hard-drive."

With a huff, she turned and poured another glass of wine before following him into the den. "How do I shred the memories, Aidan? Got any ideas on that?"

Aidan waited for her to take a seat on the couch in front of the fire. After a beat, he opted to sit beside her.

He had some ideas of how to take her mind off that, but he wasn't bold enough to kiss her again. Even with the excellent bottle of wine they'd opened for dinner.

"You're still in love with him, aren't you?"

"No."

She'd denied that a little too quickly. Another reason to avoid Cara Lamon. He wouldn't go after a woman who was in love with someone else. He didn't like playing second fiddle to a con man.

Well, he rarely went after women, anyway. They pursued him, tried to get him to open up and change, and Aidan ignored them. At which point they either tried harder or left in a huff. He could never be sure if they were attracted to him … or if they were attracted to him being a Castle.

He was no prince charming.

"Okay, so we'll avoid that subject—the being in love with him stuff. As far as I can see, I've cleaned enough to keep you safe for a while. If he decides to talk—say if he goes to a tabloid and spills the beans to turn the tables on you, then we'll have problems."

"Will this ever go away?"

"You could come clean and get through it."

"Not before the wedding. No. I mean it."

Aidan couldn't argue with that. And he'd reached his limit within the law on erasing the whole ugly affair and setting up his own scam with Trey Wellington. "Okay then. Tomorrow, I have to take care of some business for the tech store. I'll be in the office all day if you need me."

"I can take care of myself," she replied. "I'm going to call Mother first thing in the morning to tell her I'm already here and that I'm okay. She can't fly into the airport until this storm clears, so that gives me some time."

"You can only hold them all off for a few days."

"I'm good at holding people off. Or I used to be."

He could believe that. She did seem a bit cold and up-tight. But not all the time.

She lifted her hair off her neck before giving a slight shrug. "I need to make some calls myself. Everyone at the foundation thought I was going to Bali alone for business and then coming here for the wedding. They have things under control there, at least."

"Checking in would be wise, in case they've heard any differently."

He couldn't understand why she'd hidden this from everyone, but he believed this Trey person had a stronghold on her and had manipulated her with a well-practiced charisma. It happened a lot, especially to people who had a lot of money. Had she been lonely, too, considering Nico being all tied up with Eleanor and Lila caught up in wedding plans?

Cara gave Aidan one of her long, silent stares. "We're both hiding out, as I said earlier. What's your real reason?"

"I've told you my reason."

"Anyone could have installed the new security system."

"Johnny and I wanted to do it ourselves, and since the new store is nearby…"

He trailed off. "Actually, I had to get away and process this year. Eleanor's changed everything, and I'm just now catching up."

"It has been a whirlwind," she agreed, sympathy in her eyes. "But Nico is so happy, and Eleanor is amazing."

"Did it get to you, too?"

"What do you mean?"

"Did you feel so left out that Trey sounded like a breath of fresh air?"

"No." Then, "Maybe. I was alone, and things seemed to be happening for everyone around me. He showed up, and he managed to take my mind off my happy stress."

"He'd probably been casing you for months."

"That makes me feel so much better." Visibly shaking that off, she added, "But I'm truly happy for my brother and Eleanor. They are made for each other."

"Right, I get all of that and I'm happy for them, but

there's all the wedding frenzy. I wanted to be away from that for a few days. You know Johnny and Annabelle are engaged now, too, right?"

"*Sí.*" She took a long sip of wine. "Everyone is getting married."

"It seems that way."

"You don't want to get married either, right? We have that in common at least."

How did she know that about him? "Why would I? I'm not good at intimacy. I don't know how to open up to people."

Her eyes slanted up, making him think of Sophia Loren. "You're good at kissing."

Well, there it was. The one thing they'd danced around since she'd arrived here.

Aidan gritted his teeth against wanting to kiss her again. "Bad idea, but … I can't un-kiss you. I'm sorry. I shouldn't have—we shouldn't have—done that. We got caught up in the whole charade of that night."

Lifting her glass, she said, "Ah, the wine has made you mellow."

"No. Time and common sense have made me reconsider."

"But you didn't seem to mind then. Why did you keep on at it if you knew you'd regret it?"

"Why do you ask that with such accusation?"

"I think you did it on purpose, to tease me, to have some fun with a woman you scorn."

"I have never scorned you."

"But you don't like me very much."

"I do like you. I just don't know you."

"Can you kiss a person and not like them very much? Can you kiss a person and not know them very well? You seem to be good at that."

"If I recall, you kissed me first. Several times."

Her elegant shrug enticed him, and her accent sharpened like a knife down his spine. "I don't recall. I thought it was the other way around."

"You're imagining things."

"No, Aidan. I know men. You kissed me in a way that made me think you *did* like me. Or maybe it *was* the costumes. We were both playing parts, being different people. That kind of thing can be freeing. Can make people more uninhibited."

"Okay, let's go with that theory," he said, inching closer to her. "I was a gambler. Maybe I wanted to gamble that night ... with you."

"And I was Annie Oakley. Maybe I wanted to shoot someone. Yet, I kissed a gambler instead. Naughty, don't you think?"

"Or maybe you wanted to kiss someone before you ran off with Trey the Betrayer? Maybe you weren't so sure about him deep down inside ... and you needed to test the kissing theory?"

She scooted closer, her spicy scent leading the way, her eyes wide with wonder and anger. "And what is the so-called kissing theory?"

"If you kiss someone when you're supposedly in love

with someone else, maybe you're hoping it will feel different, maybe make you change your mind."

"Your theory didn't work," she replied, all fiery temper, her eyes inches from his, her mouth so near he could trace the shape of her lips with his fingers.

And because he was tired and confused and a bit angry, he said, "Let's test it again then."

He lifted her toward him and pulled her head close, his hand grabbing hold of all that luscious hair. Aidan didn't think about his actions. He wanted to punish her for kissing him that night and then leaving. Wanted to see if kissing her felt as good now as it had then. And he wanted to prove to himself that she did not affect him in any way.

But punishment turned into passion, and that made this kiss even better. She did affect him, in oh so many ways.

When she sighed and leaned closer, Aidan knew he had made another big mistake. Pulling away, he shook his head.

"Time and common sense," he said, moving to the other side of the sofa.

"Snow and wine," she retorted, getting up to pace in front of the fire.

"I have work to do."

"I'm going to my room."

They parted from round two like boxers who needed cold water splashed on their faces. She hurried out of the room, but the crackling fire only reminded him of their sizzling attraction.

He'd have to lock himself in the office until the storm outside ended. But what was he supposed to do about the storm brewing inside his soul?

Chapter Six

THE NEXT MORNING, Cara washed all the linens and folded them in a precise way that would impress even the pickiest of guests. Her mother liked things in order, and so did she.

She'd even sprayed lavender mist in all the linens closets to get rid of the musty smell of the house being closed for months at a time.

And while she wandered the halls and moved up and down the stairs, she thought about kissing Aidan. Yet again. What was happening with them? They were complete opposites, but that old saying—opposites attract—seemed to be true in this case.

Maybe she had flirted with him to loosen him up a bit, and maybe she had kissed him the first time because she figured she'd hardly ever see him again and if she did, she'd be a married woman. It had all been fun and games until she'd had her heart broken and her world turned upside down.

She'd come home to find peace and quiet. Instead, she'd found the one man who made her feel uncomfortable and unworthy. She'd toyed with Aidan for fun, but had left him behind, some serious doubts echoing after her.

Why did she want Aidan to like her? No, she wanted him to respect her and accept her the way he'd accepted her brother.

Nico charmed people, and he and Aidan had apparently become close. She could be charming, but she mostly seemed to annoy Aidan. He didn't seem to like all her theatrics. Or maybe he did, and he couldn't admit it. His kisses told the truth.

They were attracted to each other even if they didn't want to be.

Why did she care?

It had to be as old as time, a woman trying to make a man notice her even though she didn't truly care about him. A silly ritual that usually backfired. Not something she did on a regular basis.

Now she really did want him to notice her, like her, respect her, *and* be her friend, if nothing else.

But she avoided the closed door to the office, a sure sign that after last night and the heat of their kissing test, she'd either failed miserably or she'd done a fantastic job.

She would get cabin fever being stuck here with him. Not just cabin fever, but a feverish need to wipe away all the pain Trey had left with her, a need to feel again, to care again, to let go and follow her heart the way she'd always done.

But her heart was too fragile now to go from one wrong love affair to another. That wouldn't be fair to Aidan.

He'd worked long hours to save her reputation. That had to mean something. Of course, he could be doing that to win points with her brother. Or maybe Aidan actually *did* care about her.

But she wondered if he'd agreed to clear her name so he could find out about her personal life. Would he hold that over her head? Had she done anything that could make things worse?

Shy in a brooding Heathcliff way, he'd had a hard life until he'd been given the keys to the kingdom. That must have been like winning the lottery, a bit overwhelming and scary.

She, on the other hand, had always had a comfortable, worldly life but like Aidan, her parent's divorce had shattered her.

Nico and she had both acted out in ways that held them at arm's length to the world. Trey had broken through her barriers because he reminded her of her father, and he'd told her a tragic tale of his own divorced parents. A tale that had to be a lie.

Had Trey done his research on her famous father, to make sure he mimicked the Lamon traits that had caused her father to be so charming and seductive? Is that why her mother had loved Nicholas Lamon to the bitter end?

Cara's father had been charismatic, persuasive, handsome, rich, and all the other things that attracted women. Too many women. Her mother once told her that it hadn't been about the money or the House of Lamon—it had been about how he made her feel. That from the moment she'd seen him standing with her father near the stables admiring a thoroughbred horse, she knew he would be the man for her.

He'd been that man. He'd loved Lila, no doubt. But his wandering eye caused him to adore other women, too.

Cara thought about Trey. She hadn't fallen for him right away, but he had caught her attention in a way that no one else ever had. No one until Aidan.

As she remembered the day Aidan had walked into the Castle Café with Johnny Darrow and caused her to take notice, she thought about their drive to the airport. Her heart had done some funny little bumps and beats, just from being in the car with him.

But he wasn't the one for her, so why couldn't she get Aidan out of her mind?

Close confinement. Had to be that.

She could imagine loving Trey the way her mother had loved her father, if he'd been honest and real. But then, her father hadn't been honest or real. Now she had to accept that love didn't die even when the dream did.

I can't love Trey anymore. I won't repeat the pattern. I won't.

And I can't rebound right into Aidan's arms—no matter how much I want to.

But Aidan was nothing like Trey.

"*Cosa dovrei fare?*"

What should I do?

That became her prayer this morning.

Impulsively, she decided she'd go for a horseback ride in the snow.

Trying to hurry, she dressed in her riding pants and boots, then found an old wool turtleneck and a puffer jacket to keep her warm. After tugging a black wool cap over her hair, she went out the back door to find Tobias so he could help her saddle up her roan mare, Duchess. The clean, crisp air would clear her head.

AIDAN GOT UP and stretched. The yard and pasture lay in a whitewash of snow, but at least the sun shined bright again. The temperature hovered below freezing. This wouldn't melt away for a while. The weather report showed black ice and several pile-ups on the many thoroughfares through the Dallas-Fort Worth area. Messy stuff, but he did have the Jeep.

He should get in it and leave.

The house had gone quiet, which made him suspicious.

What was she up to now?

He'd heard the washer and dryer going to town in the big laundry room near the garage. Heard pots and pans and dishes clinking and banging in the kitchen. Then he'd smelled a sweet, comforting scent. Lavender and a hint of mint.

Was she making magic potions to lure him into her arms again? Or to poison him and get him out of the way for good?

Hungry, he went into the kitchen and found some chicken salad in the refrigerator with a sticky note attached: *Lunch*.

Funny that she'd only been here a little over a day and he

missed her already. Taking his coffee and a sandwich back to the office, Aidan studied the computer mock-up of the tech store, tweaking it here and there as he emailed back and forth with the architect.

The building stood lean and sleek, no wasted space, with a minimalist structure that showed off the electronics and new technology with a thorough clarity.

No clutter. No messiness. No smoke and mirrors. Just convenient little groupings where customers could try out any device they wanted to buy.

That was the way he'd described his vision to Eleanor, the architects, and the builders.

Remembering the clutter of the broken-down house they'd once lived in, Aidan could still recall his mother's shrill complaints. No one ever cleaned. No one cared about the house or the yard. She called their father a worthless drunk and incompetent. Had continually screeched she deserved better than that.

Then she'd move on to her children. Aidan and Annabelle were useless to her. They didn't care about her. They needed to be more proactive and make an impression that would last. She tried to mix them with the rich kids at school, but her efforts always backfired or made them all look pathetic.

Aidan had overcome all of that.

But now he had something to prove, and he couldn't let a broken-hearted bride who'd made a bad decision change any of that.

And yet, he worried about her.

So he grabbed his coat and hat, then headed out into the cold to find her.

SHE MIGHT BE lost.

Cara looked left and right, trying to remember which trail she'd taken. But she hadn't been here in a while, and the snow made everything seem the same. She couldn't remember the last time it had snowed this much in the state of Texas.

The beauty took her breath away.

Duchess tossed her haughty copper-colored mane, snorting with an unladylike impatience.

"I know," Cara said, her hand touching the big mare's neck. "I'm ready to turn back, too. Let me figure out which way."

Duchess lifted her regal head, her nostrils flaring toward the west where a half-frozen stream trickled through the trees. An old cabin sat back from the water. Cara and Nico used to play there when they'd come here for months in the summer, running and chasing and fishing, her big brother always reaching his hand out to her, helping her, making her hurts go away. Those were good memories. Now it seemed they passed each other and kept going. Too busy to stop and actually talk to each other.

Putting that tug of pain out of her mind, she studied the cabin. "That means the main house is to the east," she told Duchess. "We'll be home soon."

Tossing her head, the roan kicked her hooves into the rutted trail.

Cara turned Duchess back toward the house, but a sound coming from the cabin halted her. Duchess lifted her head again, sniffing the air.

A child cried out.

Cara urged her horse around. Duchess took off in a trot toward the old cabin.

Someone had to be inside.

Bringing Duchess to a halt near a sapling, Cara quietly dismounted and made her way to the side window. Brushing away snow and dirt, she peered inside.

A young woman sat holding two children. Bundled in coats and hats, they huddled under an old blanket in the corner, surrounded by aged furniture, dirt, and darkness.

And all three were crying.

Cara hurried around to the door and knocked. Cautiously calling out while making sure to sound nonthreatening, she said, "I'm Cara Lamon. I own this property. I'm coming inside, but I'm not going to hurt you. I want to help."

AIDAN SHOULD HAVE saddled one of the horses, but he hadn't ridden in a long time and he wasn't in the mood to get lost in the snow and freeze to death.

So he followed the path of fresh horse hooves, wondering why Cara had decided to go off by herself. She'd told Tobias her plans, but had neglected to inform Aidan. She obviously wanted to be away from him. And soon.

Tobias had a two-way radio, but he said she'd told him to leave her alone unless she reported to him. Apparently, Tobias wasn't as concerned as Aidan.

Angry and concerned and out here freezing to prove it, he tugged at his wool cap and marched on.

If they weren't iced in, he'd be working at the new build today and he could easily find a hotel room or rent an apartment for a few weeks. That might be the best idea. If this weather ever let up. Another round tonight would cause the temperatures to hit record lows. Near impossible to find an open road.

Checking his cell, he noticed he still had a weak signal. He could call her, but then she might assume more than he wanted her to.

He shouldn't be this worried about Cara Lamon, but she had arrived and embedded herself here, and ... the place did belong to her family. Once again, he thought of himself as an interloper.

Would he always be a nomad who'd followed a cruel mother around? He and his sister had more than paid their dues with Castle's, and now he wanted to step beyond that. He had dreams, and building this store ranked first on the list.

Right now, he had to find Princess Fancy Pants and get her safely home. The skies were growing dark again.

Aidan came around a cluster of trees. A noise had him jerking his head up from his phone to find a big horse charging toward him. Startled, the animal let out a whinny of protest.

He tried to get out of the way, but the horse reared back and one of its hooves came down across Aidan's chest.

He fell back, his eyes centered on the woman trying to control the horse. The last thing he saw before the world went black was Cara's shocked expression and wide-eyed fear.

Chapter Seven

"TOBIAS, GET HERE soon. I think I've killed Aidan, and I found a woman and two children in the play cabin."

Cara's accent kicked in along with a massive dread.

"Tobias?"

"I hear you," the old man said, his voice cracking over the walkie-talkies. Glad he'd insisted she take one, Cara held onto Aidan's arm and made sure he was still breathing. "Can you get here?"

"If I can remember the spot," he said. "I'll bring the big pickup with four-wheel drive."

"It's near the stream, to the west. Remember the old cabin? You'll see us on the path. I have to go. I need to make sure Aidan is okay."

"I thought you said you'd killed him."

"He's breathing," she replied before tossing the walkie-talkie down by her boots.

Glancing toward the cabin, she hoped the woman and her two children wouldn't try to make a run for it. She'd assured the scared girl she'd take care of them.

"Aidan?" she said, checking him for wounds. Duchess had given him a good kick and knocked the air out of him, but what if he'd received internal damage? His lungs could be collapsing, or he could have a broken rib. "Aidan?"

She checked his head, her hand moving through all that lush, rich brown hair. But she didn't find any blood on his thick wool cap or in his hair, and she didn't feel any bumps.

She hoped—prayed—that his heavy wool jacket and the thick sweater underneath had shielded him from the worst.

"Aidan, wake up. Please."

He moaned and opened his eyes, a pained scowl on his tanned, darn-near-perfect face. Squinting into the sun, he finally settled his eyes on her.

"You," he said, a loopy grin changing his expression. "Princess Fancy Pants, come to my rescue."

"Are you all right?" she asked, her heart rate easing.

"Never better. I'm staring at a vision. A beautiful one."

Then he passed out again.

Cara leaned over him. "I'm sorry. Duchess can be so ornery at times."

Aidan grabbed her arms, scaring her, fully awake now. "Ornery?"

"You're messing with me," she said. "Are you alive or not?"

"I think I've died and gone to heaven."

Slapping at him, she shook her head, hating the roller-coaster ride her emotions had taken. "You are a cruel, mean man, Aidan Castle."

"Well, you and your *ornery* horse need to watch where you're going."

"We were going for help."

Lifting his head, he groaned and held his side. "Why do you need help?"

"Not for me," she said, giving him her hand so she could help him sit up. She motioned to the cabin after he situated himself. "I found some people in there—a mother and two young children."

"What?" Shaking his head, he righted his cap. "I must still be dreaming."

"No, this is real," she said. "Tobias is on his way in one of the trucks, I hope."

Looking skeptical, Aidan cocked his head. "Cara, have you been into the champagne again?"

"I'm telling you, I found them huddling in there. She's so scared, and her children are so cold and adorable. I'm bringing them home with us."

"What? Wait?"

"They can't spend the night out here again."

"You mean, they spent the night in there last night?"

"Part of the night. They'd slept in her broken-down car, but started walking through the pasture at dawn. When she found the cabin, she took her children inside to get warm."

"They walked through the snow?"

"Yes. But they were well bundled, thankfully."

Cara heard a motor revving. "Tobias's coming. I'm going to get Marlena and her children."

"Marlena. You're on a first-name basis?"

Pushing at her hair, she said, "Yes, what is your problem?"

"Besides having the breath knocked out of me, I'm concerned you're bringing strangers into your home."

"*You're* in my home and you're a stranger."

Tobias hopped out of the heavy-duty truck. "Stop your yawing and tell me what happened."

Before Cara could explain, the cabin door opened and the woman rushed out, tears streaming down her face. "Uncle Tobias?"

Cara turned to Aidan, shock coursing through her. "Did she call him uncle?"

Aidan nodded, his eyes widening in surprise as he struggled to stand. "Did you know *that*?"

"She didn't mention it. But it explains why she came through the pasture rather than the main road."

"Marlena?" Tobias hurried toward the young woman, then wrapped her in a hug. "What in tarnation are you doing here?"

"We had to leave," the tiny woman said, her stringy dark blonde hair falling around her face. She pushed her heavy bangs away from her temple, wiping at the tears tracks on her cheeks.

Gasping, Cara grabbed Aidan's arm. His expression darkened when he caught sight of what she had. Marlena had a huge bruise over her left temple and a gash where blood had congealed.

"Did that boy do this to you?" Tobias asked, his fists clenching.

Marlena nodded, her gaze moving to her children in a warning. "We took the back way late last night, but my car broke down. We stayed in the car until first light. I found that turn-off you showed me one time, so we hiked to the cabin. I was worn out, so … we rested there. But I'm out of food." Her eyes welled up, and she shook her head. "I'm sorry."

The little girl clinging to her started crying. "Mommy."

The younger boy turned his chapped face into his mother's black coat, his sock cap crooked over his curly hair.

Tobias lifted the little boy into his arms and then tugged the girl close, his hand on her shoulder. "It's okay, pumpkin. You're safe now. Uncle Tobias's got you."

"That's Sarah Sue," Cara whispered to Aidan. "And little Nate." Shrugging, she added, "I kept her talking while we were in the cabin together. I've never met any of Tobias's many family members."

Aidan stared at the freezing family, his gaze moving over Marlena's bruised temple. He glanced back at Cara, his frown gone. But the darkness in his eyes held steady.

"Now do you understand why I have to give them shelter?"

He nodded, but didn't speak. Instead, he went to help Tobias guide them to the truck.

Cara hurried to help the little ones inside. "I'll see you back at the house. Duchess is ready to go home." She touched a hand to Marlena's heavy coat sleeve. "We'll get you some food. Make sure you're warm and safe."

When she turned around, Aidan gave her a scant smile, his dark eyes full of something she couldn't read.

"Are you okay?" she asked, still worried she'd almost killed him. "Do we need to call a doctor?"

"I've had worse injuries in bar fights," he mumbled, looking like the gambler she'd kissed. He hopped into the truck, but held the door open.

"You'll have to tell me more about that later," she suggested as she mounted her impatient horse.

Waggling her fingers in his direction, she followed the big truck back to the house.

AIDAN DIDN'T KNOW what had come over him. He sat in the den with an ice pack to his sore ribs, per Cara and Tobias's doctoring advice, and watched as Cara took charge with Marlena and her two children, finding them food and then taking them to one of the guestrooms down the hall.

When he'd woken up lying on the ground with Cara's wide, panicked gaze on him, he'd truly believed he'd been dreaming. Had he passed out or had he imagined her calling his name and touching his head, her hands warm despite the cold, her voice full of worry and fear, that slight Italian accent lilting and captivating? Her hair had cascaded out around her face like a rich reddish-brown silk, and she'd had on a ridiculous slouchy black wool cap—probably cashmere.

She *was* cashmere and diamonds with a little denim thrown in.

He couldn't accept that he was in her league now. Today's happenings had brought that all back front and center.

When he'd seen that frightened mother, bruised and battered, holding tight to her two children, something had shifted inside him. He'd remembered his mother taking Annabelle and him by the hand and holding them close.

"We're going to be all right," Caron had whispered. "We're going to a castle. A big, beautiful, fancy house. We'll be warm and safe, and we'll never have to worry about where our next meal will come from."

His mother had tried to do the right thing, but she'd gone about it in all the wrong ways. She'd left their father. Had he ever done this to her? Hit her or hurt her? Aidan didn't remember anything like that. His dad drank and she nagged, which made him drink all over again. She wanted more, always. His dad couldn't give her anything more.

Even after they've moved into the Castle estate house and they'd stood out by the pool and watched their mother marry Charles Castle, Eleanor standing nearby sullen and sad, Caron had never really been happy. She'd wanted more and she tried to get more, turning to crimes to create what she thought would one day be her empire. Had she always craved security that badly?

He only dated women in a casual, detached way because he didn't have anything more to give. Because he'd never witnessed real love until he'd watched Eleanor and Nico fall in love. Annabelle had fought against it, too, but Johnny had won her over. Or rather, she'd fought for Johnny because she'd finally figured it all out.

Something tore through him with an intense pain that left him hurting from more than bruised ribs. He wanted the kind of family Cara and Tobias seemed to have.

A family that ran toward each other instead of pulling

away. Annabelle and he had pulled away from their mother's demands and ultimatums, even when they'd both seen and heard what she might be doing. The department store became a giant maze that they moved through, invisible and unnoticed.

He'd heard things. Listened when he shouldn't have been listening. But he couldn't go against his own mother.

He'd turned away, even now finding it hard to face her. He'd mostly ignored her and her shenanigans, and he regretted that now.

Hard to deal with, but he'd come here to be alone. He hadn't had a chance to mourn for his broken family, and being isolated had always brought him a certain comfort.

You have a new family now.

He glanced up when Cara came into the kitchen, her dark sweater long over her jeans, her hair caught up in a haphazard messy bun.

She sank down on the ottoman in front of him, the one he'd sat on the other night when she'd been lying there like a crushed magnolia. In his heart, he needed to trust her. In his head, he decided he'd better not.

But the woman he'd seen today—the one who was so kind to strangers—couldn't be involved in some sort of crime, could she? Was she still covering for Trey, the man she'd loved and left?

Clasping her hands together in her lap, she said, "Tell me the truth. Are you really okay?"

"I didn't know you cared so much."

"That's not an answer."

"My ribs hurt, but I'm breathing on my own."

Except she took his breath away.

She stared at him, her eyes like a storm cloud. "Tobias is beside himself. Marlena lives on the other side of the ranch in a small cracker-box rental house. She married young, and her husband is not dependable."

"You think?"

"Tobias gave him a job here last year but most days, he didn't show up for work so he had to let him go."

"So he's unemployed and angry."

"He abuses her, and she fears for her children."

"I can understand that."

"Tobias wants to kill him."

"I can understand that, too."

"I've calmed everyone down, and the children are all cozy in bed. I found some old sweaters for them to wear while I wash what clothes they managed to bring with them. Tobias called a tow truck to retrieve Marlena's car."

He nodded, thinking she really did have a philanthropic heart. A heart she had hidden in a way that had caused Aidan to think she was a shallow, spoiled little rich girl. But this woman held a mysterious aura he longed to break through.

"I'm not letting them leave until I know they will be safe."

"This house is filling up pretty quickly," he said without malice. "How's Tobias?"

"Calm now. He sees the error of going off all half-cocked."

She was so cute when she turned Texan on him. But she

drove him wild when she turned Italian. A mixed bag of beautiful conflict.

"I won't let him go off like a vigilante cowboy," Aidan said. "Unless I'm with him."

"You two are very heroic, but we have to decide what is best for Marlena. I think the sheriff should be notified."

"Oh, well, then I'd say her husband will need to understand the consequences of his actions."

"She will not go back."

"Says you or says her?"

"She can't go back. Her children could be next."

"Tobias will take care of them?"

"Tobias and me," she said. "But for now, they rest right here. I'm going to cook. I think my mother has a beef stew recipe around here and Tobias replenished the pantry when you arrived, so I'll come up with dinner. Tobias is in the office, talking to Marlena about the possibility of her moving into the small bunkhouse near his house. It has a kitchen and bath, with a den and a bedroom. It's small, but clean and sturdy. I can give her work. We always need good workers here."

"All right," he said. "What can I do?"

"You need to rest," she said. "I can keep an eye on you from the kitchen."

"Or I can come and help you in the kitchen."

"Do you feel up to that?"

"I'll do my best. If I get tired or hurt too much, I'll kiss you and make it all better."

"You're teasing me?"

"No. I'm serious."

"We can't do that kissing thing anymore."

"We have to keep testing the theory."

"You are impossible."

"And … you are beautiful. I woke up and saw your face over me like an angel. I'm not quite over that."

"I think you hit your head on a rock since you seem a bit addled. Remember your time and common sense?"

He held a hand to his chest. "My head is clear, but my heart is hurting."

"You can thank Duchess for that."

"Right." He held his hand out to her. "Help me up."

She squinted skeptically, but offered her hand. He rose with a grimace, then tugged her close. "That's pretty cool, what you did today."

"What did I do?"

"You entertained angels unaware."

Her gray eyes softened. Became muted with emotion. But she pushed it away and moved apart from him. "Oh, I'm also entertaining a gambler, and I'm very aware."

"That makes two of us," he replied, wanting to kiss her.

But then, this could all be part of his dream.

Chapter Eight

"WHO ARE YOU?"

Aidan glanced up from his laptop to find Sarah Sue standing at the office door wearing her clean clothes, her hair freshly washed and hanging down her back in a straight silky line.

Working well into late afternoon, he'd heard laughing children and little feet running through the house, but no one had bothered him for hours.

"I'm Aidan," he replied with a tired smile. "And you must be Sarah Sue Rhodes. Or maybe you're a princess from a land far, far away."

"You're funny," she said, scooting inside the room, her boots scuffed and battered. "Do you live in this castle?"

He glanced around, thinking this house would look like a castle to someone who lived in a tiny rental.

"I'm visiting, but this isn't a real castle. It's a ranch house."

"It has a lot of rooms," she replied before plopping into one of the big leather chairs and placing her tiny hands against the arms. She lifted to turn and stare over the back of the chair. "And a lot of bookshelves."

She looked like a doll sitting there. "Do you like books?"

Sarah Sue bobbed her head, her brown eyes bright. "I'm learning to read."

"How old are you?" he asked, thinking he didn't know that much about little kids.

She held up five fingers. "I'll be six one day."

Aidan walked over to the floor-to-ceiling shelves and found the section of children's books, well-worn and tattered, but still readable.

"How about you take a couple of these? You can borrow them. Take good care of them, okay?"

She shot him a snaggle-toothed grin. "I'll bring 'em right back, too."

"Sarah Sue?"

Aidan gave her an exaggerated grimace. "Someone's looking for you."

"I'm with Hadan, Mommy."

Marlena came rushing into the office, fear in her eyes. "It's Mr. *Aidan*," she corrected, motioning to her daughter. "And you shouldn't be pestering him."

"I'm not pestering. I'm borrowing books."

"I told her she could take a couple," Aidan said, smiling at Marlena.

She appeared to be a few years younger than him. Pretty in a plain and simple way, all cleaned up and wearing some of Cara's clothes, her hair pulled back at the nape of her neck in a ponytail, her bangs covering her wounds.

"Thank you," Marlena said. "She loves books."

"So do I," he said. "And the Lamon Library has a lot of them."

Marlena thanked him again. Then she leaned over to Sarah Sue, whispering something in her ear.

The little girl stepped close, holding her books to her chest, her eyes on Aidan. "Thank you for loaning me the books, Mr. Hadan."

Laughing, Aidan leaned down. "Technically, they aren't my books, but Cara won't mind you borrowing them."

"Is Miss Cara a princess?" Sarah Sue asked.

Aidan smiled again. "Yes, she's a special princess. She's smart, funny, and she knows how to take care of herself. Just like you and your mom. Those things are what make a real princess, okay?"

"Okay." Sarah Sue grinned, her smile full of hope.

When he straightened up, he saw Cara standing outside the double doors to the office, her eyes misty with gratitude.

"Dinner is ready," she announced. Then she turned and hurried back across to the kitchen.

Cara didn't know what to think. Aidan had gone and done something nice, *and* he'd complimented her to boot. He *must* have hit his head out there. He seemed to have mellowed just enough to show he might be human.

Very human and very hunky. When he'd opened his eyes there on the snowy path, Cara's heart had lifted and resettled itself. Because he was alive and gorgeous, and he'd looked into her eyes as if she were the only woman on earth. He might be king of the geek squad, but he would always be that dark knight gambler to her.

She worried he'd fuss about their houseguests. Instead, he'd embraced Marlena and the children, giving them smiles, making jokes at the dinner table. Acting carefree and happy. What had come over the man?

He had seen her in action. Could that be it? Did he see her good side now? He finally seemed to believe she really did love her work.

She sat at the table, watching the children giggling, at Aidan and Tobias, who were smiling and acting goofy. Cara wanted this kind of life. She didn't need fame or fortune. Grateful she could take care of herself and contribute to her family's legacy through her philanthropic activities, she still wanted more. She loved helping people, but one day she'd like to have her own children laughing at the table.

Tobias winked at her from his spot at the head of this table. "Missy, you're awful quiet. What's brewing in that pretty head of yours?"

"We need a Christmas tree," she said, realization hitting her in a moody moment. "It's December, right?"

"And it's snowing," Tobias added. "Christmas is coming. Can't stop it."

Marlena's smile faded. "Christmas." She said the word with a heavy dread.

"Will Santa find us here, Mommy?" Nate asked, a chunk of biscuit in his chubby hand.

Marlena's eyes went wide. "I don't—"

"Sure he will," Tobias filled in, nodding and daring anyone to doubt him. "Santa has a built-in map in his brain. He knows all the little children of the entire world and where to find them."

"Or course," Cara said, bobbing her head. "This ranch is on his route every year."

"But we need lights and presents," Sarah Sue added. "Mommy told us we wouldn't get any of that this year."

"We don't got money," Nate added, his lower lip sticking out. "And we don't got a way to tell Santa."

Cara's gaze caught Aidan's across the table. He looked forlorn and sad as the two children.

"You don't need money to have a good Christmas," Tobias said. "And Santa—well, he hears things without you having to sit on his lap." Waving his hand toward the window, he kept at it. "We got Christmas trees all over the place. And we have decorations stored out in the barn. I'll need two volunteers to help me find a good tree first thing tomorrow."

"Me," Sarah Sue shouted, raising her hand.

"And me," Nate chimed in, grinning, gravy on his lip.

"Then that settles it," Tobias said. "We got work to do. We have to pretend we're Santa's helpers and get this place spruced up."

"Will you help, Hadan?" Sarah Sue asked, her expression full of hope.

Cara glanced from the little girl to Aidan.

He looked starstruck and shell-shocked.

"Uh … sure. I'd love to help."

"We can all go and help search for the perfect tree," Cara added. "And I know exactly where all the decorations are, so we'll drag those out and get this place ready for Santa."

Marlena's misty gaze moved over the other adults while her children giggled and chattered. "Thank you," she mouthed.

Cara smiled, realizing she hadn't thought of Trey as much today. She also realized she could help the local people around the ranch as much as she could people in third-world countries.

Her mother had always said, "When you're down, help someone who's worse off and then you won't feel so sorry for yourself."

Cara had done that very thing, many times over. She liked to help those less fortunate.

Cara glanced across the table at Aidan. His eyes held hers, his expression more settled and relaxed than ever before, that darkness she's noticed earlier gone now. Getting into the Christmas spirit might help them both to relax and forget their commitments and obligations. And their mistakes.

Had he managed to wipe away her one big mistake? She couldn't have this scandal coming out when the wedding and Christmas were both coming up.

That would be a disaster.

THE HOUSE WAS blissfully quiet.

Aidan sat in his usual spot by the fire in the big office. Snow fell in a hushed urgency, but the wind pushed the temperature below freezing. He didn't want to think about Marlena and her kids out there. What if Cara hadn't found them? They might have stayed in that hut all day and night. They could have died, cold and alone.

He heard a soft knock at the partially open door.

"Come in."

Cara pushed at the door, carrying a tray with two mugs and some cookies on it.

"I thought you might need a break."

"Hot chocolate?"

"Do you like it?"

He heard the hope in her voice. "Sure."

"I made sugar cookies."

"I happen to like cookies, too."

She set the tray on the desk. "The children are asleep, and Marlena made me leave the kitchen. She's cleaning up, and then she's going to bed."

"That explains the quiet."

"Ah, do you miss your self-imposed isolation?"

"I do, but I have to admit having kids in the house is kind of nice."

Her eyes went deep at that admission. "I can't believe you said that, or those nice things about me earlier."

"I'm not a complete Grinch," he retorted with a frown. "You did your good deed for Christmas. You took in strangers. And we've got plenty of room at this inn." Then he bit into a cookie, chewing and swallowing before continuing. "But ... we only have a few days before the next invaders arrive."

Cara gasped. "I never did call my mother. I'd better do that immediately. She should be up, and she'll want to know why I've been incognito."

When she stood, Aidan said, "You can stay here and call her on the land line. I won't listen in."

"Okay. Thanks."

Hot chocolate in hand, he went to stare out the window.

The crackling of the fire broke the silence in the room. The yard and woods resembled a standard winter wonderland.

Rare in Texas, but it happened every few years. It forced the bustling city to stop for a couple of days.

His phone buzzed. After he pulled it from his pocket, he saw a message from a friend helping him track Trey Wellington.

Call me. Found some interesting information on CL.

Cara. What had his friend found? He hated to break the fragile peace that had come with today's discoveries.

And yet, he had to know the truth. He couldn't live with secrets and lies, not the way his mother had.

Stranded. With Princess Fancy Pants.

He'd call his friend later.

Cara told Lila where she was and then went on. "Yes, I'm fine. I know I should have checked in sooner. But we'll see each other in a few days. I can't believe the wedding is almost here."

Aidan turned, and she gave him a thumbs-up from her spot on the couch. Suddenly, her eyes went wide, and he saw the panic in her expression.

"What? You're coming into Dallas early? When do you plan to arrive?" Raising an eyebrow, she mouthed to Aidan. "Two days."

Aidan shook his head. His sanctuary had become Grand Central Station. But as with the Castle estate, he felt like the interloper.

Cara jumped up and took his hand, gripping him like a lifeline. "What? Are you sure? Eleanor and Nico are coming home early, too? But Mother, it's snowing here."

After that, she lapsed into Italian and Aidan drained his hot chocolate, wishing he had something a little stronger.

This party was about to get started. He'd have to keep tabs on things, so Cara wouldn't be exposed before the big day.

But how bad could it be if they did find out?

Pretty bad, he figured. He didn't like her tactics, but he'd stand by her and keep her secrets. For now. Or at least until he had the whole story and the findings to show her innocence. Aidan prayed he had made the right decision. He couldn't tell her he was investigating her, too.

She'd kick him out of her life. And he wasn't ready for that to happen.

Because her cookies were almost as good as her kisses.

Chapter Nine

CARA'S WORLD KEPT spinning out of control. But she'd promised the Rhodes children they'd have Christmas, and she aimed to make that happen. So here she stood in the early morning cold. She had two days before her mother, Nico, and Eleanor showed up back in Dallas. She'd worry about that when they got here. Too early and way too frigid to try to keep all the plates spinning.

"We're ready," Nate said as he rammed into Cara's leg and held her tight. "A twee. A twee."

"You're right on time," she replied, trying to be merry and bright, but still bleary-eyed from sitting up to late working to get things in order. They had food, thankfully. Tobias had been stocking the freezer and pantry for weeks in anticipation of the wedding. She'd explain this situation to her mother, and Lila would agree she had done the right thing by taking in Marlena and her children. But Cara did not want to tell her mother about Trey and the almost-wedding until Nico and Eleanor were off on their honey-moon.

The plan had been that Eleanor's faction would stay at the Castle estate where the bachelorette party would take place, and the extra Lamons were to stay here at the ranch with Nico. On the big day, the bride's party would all gather at Castle's to get dressed in the apartment and the secret dressing room next to it, where Tiffany would do their hair and makeup. Eleanor and her bridesmaids would then leave the store to go to the park by the lake. Nico and his groomsmen would stay here and have a Texas-style barbecue bachelor party the day before the wedding, then the next day come into town and meet them at the Dallas Arboretum where the wedding would take place.

The best-laid plans.

She had checked online and so far, nothing new or scandalous about her had popped up. In fact, other than a few articles about her work, she couldn't find anything about herself. Aidan had done a good job. Shutting down social media accounts was one thing. People took a break from that all the time. But trying to find those little tidbits of juicy scandal and clear them away was a hard assignment.

Trey probably knew how to bypass all of that.

Aidan had warned her not to google Trey. He could pick up on that and find her. But he had to know she'd be here for her brother's wedding, so what did it matter?

She'd think about this later.

But she hoped he hadn't been able to get to the money she'd set aside from foundation funds to foster his "orphanage". She had to accept that the only charity Trey cared about would be his own.

"Cara?"

Aidan stood next to her wearing a cowboy hat and a heavy suede jacket, his jeans worn, his boots dark brown burnished leather. "Are you ready?"

"Yes," she replied, her heart tripping over her pulse.

"Are you okay?"

"Yes," she repeated. "Just … thinking about my to-do list."

"I checked on some things this morning," he said on a low whisper, his eyes searching her face. "I think the anonymous notice I put out over the net has Trey on the move. It hit several feeds, and people are sharing it enough that it's trending everywhere. The worse thing in the world for a con artist is to have people comparing notes on him."

"Did you have to open with that bit of depressing news?"

"Do you want me to keep it from you?"

"No."

His expression moved from worried to distrustful. He still wasn't sure about her. And why should he be? She couldn't trust herself these days. Had she done something, slipped up somewhere?

"We'll talk later." He turned and followed Tobias to the big truck. "Right now, we have to find a Christmas tree."

Marlena and the two children ran ahead, Sarah Sue and Nate laughing and chattering away.

Cara watched the tiny group pile into the front of the double-cab truck.

Aidan gave her a lopsided grin. "Guess we get the bucket seats."

Cara thought about the tight space in the bench seat behind the front seats. "I can walk."

Aidan grabbed her arm. "You will not walk. You'll sit by

me."

"I don't have to follow your command," she retorted.

"I don't have to let you freeze on principle," he shot back. "Get in the truck."

Shivering, she glared at him. But she got inside the warm truck anyway.

Aidan climbed in beside her, his long legs practically touching his chin. "Cozy."

"Very."

The heat radiated around her, his heat. Body warmth—the best kind. She wanted to sigh and lean her head against the suede of his jacket. But instead, she sat rigid and frozen, wondering how she'd gone from a bridal gown and a jet plane to snow boots and a truck full of forced-together people.

"What am I going to do about my mother?" she whispered close to his collar.

"You could tell her the truth. Keeping secrets is hard work," Aidan said into her ear, his breath warm and smelling like fresh mint. "My mother did that, and look where it got her."

"Do you still think I'm hiding something, Aidan?"

"Do you have something to hide, Princess Fancy Pants?"

"I don't know," she admitted. "I'm so confused. I truly don't know."

Aidan's dark eyes held hers. The truck bounced and rocked while Elvis sang "Blue Christmas" on the radio. Tobias hit a rut, and Cara bounced against Aidan. He lifted his arm to hold her as she fell against him, wincing as she hit somewhere near his bruised ribs.

"That was fun," Nate shouted.

Sarah Sue giggled. Marlena smiled. Tobias shot a sage glance in the rearview mirror.

Cara tried to readjust herself, but Aidan held her there in the crook of his arm. "One day, I'm going to find out all of your secrets."

Cara shivered against the warmth pouring through her.

The kissing theory rang loud warnings inside her head while Elvis lamented being lonely on Christmas. She knew the feeling.

"One day, maybe I'll find out your secrets, too," she said, her gaze holding his.

Aidan let her go, turning to stare out the window.

"THAT'S A MIGHTY big tree," Tobias said two hours later.

Aidan stood with Tobias and Nate out by the barn, staring up at a cedar that had to be at least nine feet tall.

"Where we gonna put it?" Nate asked, his head as far back as he could get it, his eyes squinting.

"In the big den," Aidan replied. "That's the only room big enough for this tree. It has high ceilings and the biggest fireplace."

"For Santa," Nate replied with a knowing nod. The he put his hands across his chest, mimicking Aidan.

"Okay," Tobias said, tugging at the collar of his old barn jacket. "We got to shape this into something pretty."

Alternating between a hand saw and a small chainsaw, Tobias went to work while Aidan and Nate had cleanup duty. Nate grinned and chattered away, giving Aidan time to think about what his friend had told him last night when he'd finally called him back.

Aidan had met Paul Wade in college. Paul had gone into finance and now worked as a financial investigator, but they had stayed in touch. Paul had gone back to college as an adult. He was ten years older than Aidan, and a great mentor at advising him on just about anything in life. Aidan had brought him in after Eleanor had exposed his mother's white-collar crimes. Paul had been honest with him then, telling him Caron was guilty and she would be prosecuted unless she took the deal Eleanor's lawyers offered her. Aidan needed him to be honest with him about Cara, too.

"Tell me everything."

"Trey Wellington is a real piece of work. He has several aliases, and I'm sure as many passports. This isn't the first time he'd conned a woman, but he usually goes for older women, widowed and wealthy ones usually. He never offers to marry them, but he befriends them and persuades them to invest in his nonexistent schemes."

"Why hasn't he been caught?"

"He hides in plain sight and has a lot of people fooled. They vouch for him. It's kind of weird, but you know how this works. He's a classic example of a career criminal. And yes, he's a psychopath."

"Do you think he could be dangerous?"

"If he's cornered, yes. He'll find a way to get to that

money."

"Why did he target Cara?"

"I think the man really liked her, but … you know money is his first love. From what I can dig up, he saw her at a charity event in London. Had to have been casing other women. I found one blurry picture of him following her around a room. I'm guessing he went after her, studied up on the Lamon fortune, and decided he wanted to get in on that and maybe added in the Castle connection, too. He might have really wanted to marry her, but he also wanted the money. Marrying her would have given him a home base to continue his work. He's trying to get to the money she transferred from one bank to another. So far, no go."

"Where is the money?"

"In a bank in Milan with tight security. Again, in plain sight."

"What else? You said you had information on Cara?"

"Yes. This money came from Lamon Foundation funds as she said, but the word on the street is that she took it on purpose, so she could run away with Wellington."

"Why would she do that? She has an impressive trust fund, and her family is stable and wealthy. Not to mention, the foundation money is tightly controlled and carefully handled."

"Your friend is rumored to be a serial fiancée who could possibly be robbing from the foundation to keep up with the men she almost marries."

"Excuse me?"

"She has a pattern of falling in love with the wrong men,

but breaking things off before they go too far."

Aidan remembered that Cara had admitted that. "She told me about that. Men want her money. She can't trust them. And her brother is, of course, very protective of her."

"Understandable," Paul said. "I don't think her cold feet is an issue. Not much publicity on that. Just some blurbs in the gossip magazines and online social sites. But if Wellington is half as good as I think he is, he'd take advantage of that pattern and add a few embellishments."

Aidan had digested that news, remembering some of the details he'd found in his own searches. "Well, being skittish about getting too involved with someone isn't a crime."

"But taking money that belongs to the foundation is. I haven't verified this, but Trey is putting out the word that she uses foundation money for her own purposes. And that he has proof because she used funds while with him."

Aidan didn't buy it. "Why would she do that? The Lamons are wealthy."

"But there was a time a few years ago when they almost lost everything. That's a well-documented fact."

Aidan didn't argue with that. He knew the story of how their father had almost lost the entire business. Nico had come home after his father's death to bring it back from the brink.

"And you think Cara now hides money because she's afraid this could happen again?"

"I don't think that, but Trey Wellington is spreading rumors. And we both know that one rumor can ruin any philanthropic organization, and cause investigators like me to be brought in to find out the truth."

"The Lamon Foundation could be audited," Aidan said, thinking Trey wanted revenge. "Do you know where she might be hiding any other money, if she is doing that?"

"Can't find a trace, but I can find out if she's leading a double life. Want me to stay on it?"

"Yes, and so will I."

Aidan had ended the call more confused than ever. Trey had a reason to make Cara look bad, but he also had been close to her for the last few months. Had she confided something to him that he could now use against her? She'd told Aidan she liked to keep a low profile. Was that why she didn't want any accolades or publicity? Was she afraid someone would find she'd been embezzling money?

This could not be happening again, could it?

Stopping now to answer something Nate had asked, Aidan rubbed his eyes and stared up at the big ranch house. He wouldn't go through this again. Just being associated with this could ruin things for him with the new technology store. Eleanor would be furious with them both, and Nico would flip.

He wouldn't believe this until he had the proof in his hands. The Cara he had come to know wouldn't risk something like this. Would she?

And if he point blank asked, would she tell him the complete truth?

"THIS IS A beautiful tree."

Cara stood back to admire their handiwork, her heart filling with something she couldn't quite put her finger on. She'd been in on tree decorations before, but this one seemed so special. Seeing the smiles on Sarah Sue and Nate's faces made all the difference. She'd always wanted to help other people. Being the head of the Lamon Foundation allowed her to do that. Trey could ruin it for her, and now Aidan was acting weird. Was that because of the kissing theory, their jammed-together ride this morning, or did he think she hadn't confessed everything?

She didn't have time to ponder her own questions.

"It's the best tree ever," Sarah Sue squealed, bringing Cara out of her thoughts. "Santa will love this!"

"Of course he will," Tobias replied, his lips smacking with pride. "Santa will give us the grand prize."

"What's the grand prize?" Nate asked, his expression so precious Cara wanted to hug him close.

"Big stockings," Tobias replied, his hands spread wide.

"Full of things?" Nate asked.

"All kinds of things," Cara replied, thinking she'd have to do some fast online ordering. Only she wasn't supposed to be online right now. Trey could trace her.

Marlena didn't speak. She stood in awe, staring at them while she wiped her eyes.

Focusing on the here and now, Cara shifted gears. "Okay, we've finished the tree."

Gazing over at Aidan, she poked him with her elbow. "What do you think?"

Shaking his head, he stared up at the gold, white, and silver ornaments mixed in with treasured favorites and colorful twinkling lights. "That tree is so loaded it will probably topple over."

He didn't sound that impressed. Distracted. He sounded distracted, and that made her gnaw at her bottom lip with worry.

How would she ever get through the wedding and the holidays when she didn't know what might happen next? She had a bad feeling *Aidan* might be keeping something from *her*.

"Let's finish this house," she said, pushing away her fears like she'd always done. "Full speed ahead."

Aidan glanced at her, his dark eyes showing her nothing while they made her feel so exposed.

"Are you all right?" she asked as the kids tugged decorations out of boxes, Marlena supervising with motherly tones of encouragement.

"Never better."

"You'd tell me if anything was wrong, right?"

"I'd tell you anything you need to know, yes."

"Not a good answer."

"Not the right question."

So they were back to sparring and circling.

The pressure might break Cara. Suddenly, she wished her mother was here right now.

Chapter Ten

EXHAUSTED, CARA SAT down on the big sofa in the living room, a cup of hot tea in her hand. It was midnight, and she had one more day before her mother arrived. Lila would take charge. Maybe then, Cara could finally have some time to herself. The weather man said the snow would be gone in a couple of days, but the temperatures wouldn't get much above freezing.

The wedding was only a few days away now, so she hoped that prediction would change and the ice would melt. Thankfully, the seamstress at Castle's had her bridesmaid dress ready and waiting. But her heart seemed lost somewhere between Trey Wellington and Aidan Castle.

As if she'd conjured him up with her thoughts, Aidan walked through the wide arched opening from the main hall and gazed at her, his big frame blocking the muted light from the hallway.

"Hi," she said, her voice a whisper.

"Hi." He came and sat down beside her, his fatigue obvious from the dark circles underneath his eyes.

Cara gave him a report. "Tobias is at his place, and Marlena and the children have gone to bed. Tomorrow, I'll show them the bunkhouse next to Tobias's. He's cleaned it, and he checked to make sure the water and electricity are working. Meanwhile, we have this beautiful tree, but I still somehow have to let Santa know I need clothes and toys, lots of both. What a day."

His eyes moved over the tree before settling on her. "Yes, what a day. You've been busy, and you're a great hostess. Thought of all of their needs. A lot of busy work to keep your mind off Trey Wellington."

The way he said it almost sounded like an accusation. Did he think she kept busy while things stalled in her personal life?

Okay, so maybe she did tend to push away unpleasant situations. Did that bother him?

"You're right. I haven't thought much about him since Marlena and the children showed up. But I had to do something to help them."

She didn't tell Aidan that her mind had been on *him* more now, too. Which only made her determined not to follow the same pattern of loving, losing, and starting right back up.

Even if this one appeared so very different.

Aidan took in her words and gave her that winged eyebrow stare, his big arms folded over his chest in a warrior stance. "We've been here three or so days, and it's been wild. But we still have the problem of Trey and his dirty business."

"What have you found, Aidan? Because I think you're not telling me everything."

He reached out and touched a strand of her hair, twirling it around his finger. "Trey is on the move, and he's trying to get to the money. A few nibbles, but nothing substantial with the post I sent out. I've always heard con men can get their victims to vouch for them. I need to know if you have any other funds hidden elsewhere, and if you've ever told him about any other secret, protected bank accounts."

Cara pulled away and stood up, remembering days gone by. She'd always been good with money, but would he understand the folly of her youth? Better to let that slide for now.

"No, of course not. Whenever I invest in any non-profit endeavor, I always move the funding to the bank I told you about. It's a holding fund that moves either into the charity's funds or goes directly to the people we've agreed to sponsor. It works like a funnel, so we can keep each organization's spending needs separate and accounted for."

Aidan stayed on the sofa, seeming fascinated with the twinkling tree. "Does anyone else from your organization have access to this money?"

"No. Not without me. My assistant Jennifer Savanti stays on top of this, along with several accountants. But I give the final word by signing off on bank transfers. Why do you ask?"

"Does your assistant know where you are right now?"

"No. Jennifer thinks I went to Bali. Alone. Before I came here to get ready for the wedding. I haven't alerted her that I arrived early."

Handing her his phone, he said, "Check in with her. Ask her if she's had any calls that seem off-course."

"Do you think Trey's trying to get in touch with her?"

"He could be. I don't know. It's a guessing game at this point."

She stood still, studying him. He seemed tense and wound up. But then, his life had been disrupted in so many ways. He'd had a shower and he smelled like the woods in summer, his hair damp and inky. Cara had to swallow back the ache in her heart. It would be so easy to fall into Aidan's arms and let him hold her. But she was determined to stop being a serial falling-in-love-type woman.

"Trey wouldn't dare try to get to my employees. I have always kept my personal life separate from my work. Jennifer only knew I was involved with someone, but she also knew to be discreet. I didn't tell anyone about the wedding."

Shrugging, she added, "Besides, I moved around in the dating circles like a magpie, always searching for something or someone, and I wanted things to be different this time. I didn't want my family to nag me, and I didn't want my assistant or the others who work with me to get their hopes up about my love life yet again."

"So you finally made it this far—to the wedding—and you still didn't want to let anyone know?"

"I thought Trey was that someone I'd been waiting for. When he also wanted to keep things low-key and secret, I readily agreed."

She wasn't proud of it, but Aidan needed to know. She would try very, very hard not to take things any further with him either. "My mother and brother want me to settle down, but I felt smothered and patronized. So yes, I kept it a secret the same way I've always protected my privacy. My delicious

LENORA WORTH

secret. My biggest mistake."

"Why do you feel the need to be so secretive?" he asked, his eyes meeting hers.

Shocked and hurt because he didn't seem to believe her and he'd posed the question as in the here and now, she said, "For the same reasons you like to hide out here in the country. I like my privacy. I work hard and put on a smile every day, but I've also seen the worst of life. I have seen orphans in Africa and children in the slums of India. I know what happens when war ravages a country and people become refugees."

She pushed her hand through her hair, agitated. "And … I've been threatened, too many times to count."

He sat forward, his hands cupped together. "Trey's going to make his move, Cara. He'll go through anyone he can get to, and he'll try every maneuver to transfer that money. Check in with your assistant."

She used his phone to leave a message for Jennifer, then turned to Aidan. "We're seven hours behind them. It's early morning there, so she's probably not in the office yet. But maybe she'll check her messages and call me back since I told her no matter the time."

Aidan patted the sofa. "Okay, come sit down and try to relax."

"Easy for you to say." Instead, she turned to the fire, wanting to tell him the same thing. "I love summer. I want summer back."

"Don't we all?"

"You're an introvert, aren't you?" she said over her

106

shoulder.

"How did you guess?" he said on a dry drawl.

She twisted to grin at him, thinking she really did like the man. Funny in a serious kind of way and so handsome in a nerdy way, he had on black reading glasses that would have looked silly on any other man. On him, though, they looked good. Too good.

He took them off, appraising her. "You like life, don't you? I mean, you love being out around people?"

"Yes. But once I'm done, I like a little downtime." Shrugging, she said, "Our parents' divorce was all the news in the fashion world. I lost friends, and I learned the cruelty of life. I was a social butterfly type who quickly became a recluse. I did some things I'm not proud of, but once I went away to college, I got my life back on track. That, as well as the way our parents stayed friends, helped me a lot." She wanted to tell him the whole story, but she needed him to finish this first.

"So, having been deceived, you came here to figure things out and we've all messed with your plans?"

"No," she said, finally giving in to sitting next to him. "Trey messed with my plans. I could be with him in Bali right now, clueless and happily married."

"He would have broken your heart."

"He's already done that."

"I've never had my heart broken. I think I've protected it too much."

"I've heard you like to flirt, but you never commit."

"Who told you that?"

"Your sister."

"Ah, you and she have become close. You told her about Trey."

"Yes, but I never gave her his name."

"No, but after she noticed that you and I seemed to—what did she call it? Oh yes, have it bad for each other—I told her that we weren't meant for each other."

Cara twisted to glare at him. "Did you tell her we kissed?"

"No. I don't kiss and tell."

She could believe that about him. "I should call Annabelle."

"Bad idea."

"Why? She and I are friends. She can console me in my time of need."

"She's with Johnny now."

"Do you resent that? Does it mean she's not allowed to talk to us?"

"No, it's not that. I don't want to disrupt her happy vibes."

"I'd be a disruption."

"I'm saying this all wrong."

Studying him, Cara huffed a laugh when clarity dawned. "You don't want her to know you're here with me."

Sheepishly, he nodded. He was too cute. Cara wanted to do some heavy cuddling. "She'd pester us both and make life unbearable. She already thinks I have the hots for you."

"Do you?"

He stared over at her, eyes heavy-lidded. The tree twinkled and blinked. The fire hissed and danced. Cara's heart did all the above.

Waiting, she held her breath. Saw the same war she was fighting battling inside him. Cara didn't dare move.

But then he moved closer to pull her into his arms, settling his mouth firmly against her own.

Cara fell into the kiss, giving up the game because he was big and warm and she felt secure in his arms. He might be a dark knight, but he was *her* dark knight.

Stars sparked behind her eyelids, but then he broke the kiss. He didn't let her go, only pulled her tighter against him. "Rest, Princess Fancy Pants. We have a tree and a fire, and we're still stranded. Might as well make the most of it while we can."

Cara snuggled even deeper into his arms, and he grabbed a chenille comforter and wrapped it around them. She had so much to worry about but for now, she felt safe and protected, his kisses covering her like this soft blanket.

Aidan didn't want or need her money. But he did need someone to show him what a kind and good man he'd become despite it all.

She might be that person, if her life wasn't in such a mess right now.

Please let us get through the wedding, she prayed. *After that, I'll do my best to prove to him that I'm not a horrible person.*

She didn't think she'd rush away from this man. Because he wasn't after anything other than this. They both needed the solitude of cuddling by a fire on a snowy night.

So she drifted off to sleep in his arms. The best sleep she'd had in days.

THE PHONE SENT out an annoying buzz.

Cara came awake, extracting herself from the warmth of Aidan's arms. They'd fallen asleep on the couch, her tucked against his side, him with his head against hers.

"It's Jennifer," she said, already missing his warmth.

Aidan sat up, rubbing his eyes before glancing at his watch.

"*Ciao*, Jennifer," Cara said in a groggy voice.

"Sorry to wake you," her assistant, American and very proper, said. "But you asked that I call you at this number no matter the time."

"That's okay. I'd fallen asleep on the couch. Don't worry about the late hour," Cara replied, glancing at Aidan. He looked all sleepy and gorgeous, his hair disheveled and his five-o'clock shadow way past five o'clock. "I need to ask you a few questions."

"Okay," Jennifer replied. "Are you in Texas now?"

"Yes, but I've got some people watching the Wellington account."

"Oh, yes. The orphanage in Botswana, right?"

"Yes. The remaining funds are in our holding account. I had planned to transfer them later this week, but I've decided to wait on that project."

"Hmm," Jennifer replied. "I had someone call about that

both yesterday and today."

"Who called?" Cara asked, turning to nod to Aidan.

"A man who said he represented the Well-and-Wind Orphanage. He expressed concern because the funding hadn't been wired yet. I told him I'd check in with you if I could locate you. But we got very busy with the holidays coming. I didn't want to bother you while you were in Bali. I'm sorry."

Closing her eyes, Cara tried not to scream. The Well-and-Wind had been Trey's big project. It probably didn't even exist. Or if it did, he had to have been using an established organization to fool her.

"You did the right thing. I can't deal with this right now, so it will have to wait until after my brother's marriage. I'm having doubts about this endeavor."

"So if anyone calls, I should stall?"

"Yes, please. We will hold off until after the wedding, no matter what anyone else tells you. Understand?"

"Is something wrong?" Jennifer asked.

"I don't know yet, and I can't talk about it until I have more information. Thank you for alerting me. I'll check back in later. Please call me if anyone else gets in touch about this matter." Then she added, "By the way, do you have the representative's number?"

"Yes. I can pull it up from my contacts. I'll text it to you."

"Thank you, Jennifer. I might be able to handle this from here after all. Anything else?"

Jennifer hesitated. "Nothing urgent. I'll keep you posted."

After Cara hung up, she stared at Aidan. "I think Trey tried to call my office."

"Not Trey," Aidan said. "He had someone call for him. But if he can't get information that way, he will show up there and try to charm anyone he can."

"You mean Jennifer?"

"She's a woman, right?"

"That's an unnecessary reminder."

"It's the truth. He goes after women."

She couldn't argue with Aidan. "She's sending me the phone number, but from what you say it won't matter."

"No. Probably a burner. Can't be traced."

"Is this ever going to end?" she asked, tired down to her bones.

He tilted his head, his bangs going along for the ride. "You're not giving up, are you?"

"Shouldn't I?"

He got up, then turned her toward the hallway. "Go get some sleep, Princess Fancy Pants. I've got your back."

Cara allowed him to guide her to her bedroom door. "Do you still doubt me?"

"I'm learning not to doubt you, but this is going to be hard to shake. You need to tell me anything you might remember or ... know."

"I've told you everything."

"Okay then."

Leaning in, he kissed her forehead. "I'll keep trying to find Trey, so we can end this nightmare."

"Thank you. After this is over, the wedding is done, and we can relax, I'm taking you out for a celebratory dinner."

"After this is over and the wedding is done, I'm going to find a private island," he replied. He held her there against the door, his gaze moving from her eyes to her lips. "And I might just take you with me."

Chapter Eleven

"AIDAN, WHERE HAVE you gone? To Siberia?"

His sister almost sounded concerned. Six days in with Cara—and now Tobias, Marlena, and the children—and he hadn't bothered calling anyone to come rescue him.

"I told you, Annabelle, I'm stuck here at the ranch in this snow and ice."

"Aren't you lonely?" she asked, her tone so full of giddy he wanted to throw up.

"I'm not lonely." And he certainly wasn't alone.

Shutting the office door so she wouldn't hear the pitter-patter of little feet or the throaty Italian voice of Cara Lamon, Aidan rubbed his eyes. "I've been working from home, monitoring the build site. But with this weather, things have grinded to a halt."

"The whole city has grinded to a halt," Annabelle replied. "I'm worried about the wedding."

Aidan wasn't worried. "You know Nico and Eleanor. They'll get married if they have to do it inside Castle Department Store."

"Perish the thought," his dramatic sister said. "We've worked too hard to set up the perfect venue."

"In December, in the middle of winter."

"But you and I both know December in Dallas is usually mild compared to other parts of the country. Besides, the park is their special place."

"Tell that to the weatherman," he retorted, staring out at the patches of snow still left in the yard.

Annabelle changed the subject. "So, Johnny says you two installed a new security system at the ranch. How's that working?"

"We still have some kinks in the system." Cara and her hammer came to mind.

"But you'll be able to get into town for the wedding, right?"

"That's the plan. I'll do my part as one of the grooms-men, under duress, of course. The roads are beginning to clear." Then he asked, "Where are you?"

"I'm at the estate house for now. Johnny is at his house, but he's keeping tabs on the store, of course."

"Is it shut down?"

"Unfortunately, since downtown Dallas looks like a ghost town. We're losing Christmas shopping days, but we'll make it up to our customers when this weather clears."

"You sound like a true Castle now, little sister."

"I feel like a true Castle," she admitted. "It's a good feel-ing. The Lone Star store in doing well beyond expectations, and I'm enjoying training the visual merchandising staff. Kimmie is going to make a great manager one day."

"Kimmie, the young girl you took under your wing?"

"Yes. In other words, me at that age."

Glad that his sister was on the right track *and* the fast

track, Aidan wondered what would have happened to them if Eleanor had never come home.

He didn't want to think about that. "It's been a year. I think I needed some downtime."

"You always have needed to debrief after too many changes."

"And you always wanted to party. Things have changed, but in a good way."

They chatted a few more minutes, and he again assured his sister he was fine. Before he could end the call, the office door opened and Cara walked in unannounced.

"Aidan, I need to talk to you—"

Wincing, he put a finger to his lips.

Annabelle gasped. "Aidan Castle, do you have a woman there with you?"

He wouldn't lie, but he had to protect Cara's privacy, too. "That is none of your concern, sister."

"Snowed in with a mysterious woman," Annabelle said on a near squeal. "You never cease to surprise me, Aidan."

"Got to go," he said, ending the call before she could grill him. Sighing, he sat back against the desk and faced Cara.

"I'm sorry," Cara said, making a face. "Does she know you're with me?"

"No. But if I know Annabelle, she'll put things together."

"I don't mind her knowing. We're not together-together, and she needs to know so she won't misunderstand."

Giving Cara a stern stare, he shook his head. "We've got

enough problems without Annabelle sticking her skinny nose into our business." Brushing a hand over his hair, he said, "What did you need to talk about?"

"I thought of something," she said, the scent of her flowery shampoo lifting the stuffy gloom of the office.

"And?"

"Trey claimed to have an apartment in New York."

"And you just now remembered this?"

"Yes, I just now remembered because he only mentioned it once in passing when I told him I would be coming to Dallas for the costume ball and the Lone Star Castle's opening."

"Did he suggest you stay in his apartment on the way?"

"No, he suggested we'd go that far together, then he'd stay in New York for business and I could come to Dallas."

"But you didn't do that?"

"No. I needed an earlier flight than the one he wanted. He liked to do the red-eye a lot."

"In first-class and even more private, no doubt."

She rolled her eyes at that. "Yes."

"Did you fund his travels?"

"No. He had plenty of money for traveling. But I already told you I did pay for a few things out of kindness, and … well … that whole being in love delusion I held."

"The amount you named indicates you footed some heavy bills for him."

"I regret that," she admitted. "But that's my money to lose. I do, however, want the foundation's money back. I moved it in good faith and had all the proper paperwork done, but I'm liable for it. Trey could accuse me of embezzlement."

Aidan let that go and said, "He made it look as if he had plenty of money."

"Are you going to check on the apartment in New York or not?"

"Do you have an address?"

She rattled off a high-end address in Midtown Manhattan. "He said it had wonderful views of Central Park."

"Did he tell you those views sometimes run for close to ten million dollars, and that it's a two-bedroom and bath?"

"How do you know such things?"

"My mother always wanted a pied-a-terre in New York. She had me research several for her."

"Trey wanted to take me there. That's all I remember."

"I'm going to check it out," Aidan said. "I think for now we've got things contained, but he's going to try and get to that money one way or another." Letting out a breath, he added, "And Cara, he'll try to mess with your reputation, too. Do damage to your character. As payback for leaving him before he could marry you."

"I'll deal with that once we find him. Any action on your fake accounts?"

Aidan wouldn't lie. "Yes. A couple of women think they might remember him. But a lot of people are on his side. I'm waiting to see if anyone else puts up a picture of him."

"Can I look?"

"No. If he gets a whiff of you nosing around, he'll figure things out. He has to know you're here, but he'd be stupid to try to get to you."

"Maybe he'll go far away."

"You can't keep burying your head in the sand, Cara. Or in this case, the snow."

"You're so witty," she replied, but he saw the fear in her eyes. Then he saw the grit. "Do you honestly think I'm doing that? Once the champagne cleared, so did my head. You've helped me a lot, and I've been in touch with my own investigators and my lawyer. The money is safe for now, Aidan. It's in an untraceable account."

"What?" Aidan rose from the desk. "Did Trey suggest that?"

"Yes, but I've done this before with huge amounts of money. I told you, Nico watches me like a hawk, as big brothers do. Sometimes I have to dodge him, so I have my ways."

"Illegal ways?"

"Of course not. I deal with other people's money all the time. I wouldn't risk that."

"So you hid this money because you were also hiding your groom?"

"Yes, for the reasons I've stated over and over. Nico loves me, but he's too protective. And … I didn't want to make a big deal about my personal life because Nico would have gone off the rails with questions."

"What if you told your brother the truth?"

"Not before the wedding," she said, irritation rising in her words. "I won't do that to Nico and Eleanor. You said much the same yourself."

"This could blow up in your face, Cara. Trey could make something happen before the wedding or during the wedding."

"You're scaring me."

"I don't mean to scare you, but you need to think this through, work with me on these details, and you need to be honest with your brother." Going around the desk, he placed his hands on the calendar pad and leaned down. "I wish I'd followed through on my doubts about my mother. I could have saved her a lot of disgrace by waylaying her and talking her out of her crimes. I would have forced her to make things right. She could have left Castle's before Eleanor found out the truth."

"Because that's who you are. You want to make things right with Eleanor, your sister, and your mother, and you don't want to let Nico and Eleanor down."

"I don't want to let anyone down, especially you."

"I feel the same way," she said, putting her hands over his on the desk. "I don't want to hurt anyone or cause another scandal. I'm trying to avoid that. Just for another week or so, and then I'll tell Nico everything."

"You're playing a dangerous game."

"But you're helping me. I had planned on ignoring everything, and then going home to fix it after the holidays. You made me see that would be a big mistake."

"This isn't something you can ignore," he pointed out.

"No, and my mother will be here late tonight. I'll tell her, I promise."

"Okay." He breathed, exhaled. "The roads are clear now,

so I'm going to the technology store to see if anyone has been able to work on the finishing touches."

She lingered, a hand to her hair. "Would you mind if I come with you? I'm getting cabin fever."

"What about Marlena and the children?"

"Tobias had taken them to his place for a while. He's watching Nate and Sarah Sue while Marlena finishes her new home."

"I thought you wanted to oversee that."

"I did, until she told me to come home and rest."

Aidan grinned. "You were bossing her and making unsolicited suggestions, right?"

"Trying to help. But she's too nice to shove me out the door."

"So you took the hint and left?"

Cara's gaze slid over his face. "She gave me a big, pointed hint. She said I should come and check on you."

He absorbed that, wondering why everyone thought they had a thing. "As you can see, I'm fine. But yes, I have cabin fever, too. This has been a long week."

"And you're itching to get to your project site."

"Yes."

"I'll find something to do," she said, turning to leave.

Against his better judgment, Aidan snagged her arm with his left hand and hauled her close. "I didn't say you couldn't come."

Cara poked her finger in his still-sore chest area. "Well, you didn't jump up and down and say, 'Yes, Cara, please come with me'."

"Let's get out of here," he replied, grabbing his hat and coat. "We should be safe in the Jeep."

Her eyes went wide. "Or we could take Nico's Jag. He likes me to drive it when I'm here, you know, to keep it in shape."

"I am not taking that car. It costs more than the house I grew up in."

"He won't mind. And you did say the roads are clear, right? Besides, it has seat warmers, Bluetooth, and GPS. Does your Jeep have any of that?"

"No. It barely has a top and windows, and it could use new tires."

"Jag or Jeep?" she asked, her hands teetering like scales while she weighed the options.

"I say Jeep."

"I say Jag."

Again, against his better judgment, he agreed. "Okay, but I'm driving."

CARA NOW WISHED she'd thought their mode of transportation through a little more. Being in the two-seater with Aidan might give her heart palpitations. Too close. Kissing and touching close. But this car lived up to its name, moving through the back roads like a pouncing cat.

"The roads seemed to have cleared," she said to make conversation. "And you have to admit, this car is a dream."

"Yes, a dream I shouldn't be driving."

"But I-635 is open. That's a good thing."

"And parts of I-20."

Cara had to come up with less boring topics. "Do you like the car?"

Downshifting, he grinned. "What's not to like? It's a perfect driving machine, and we shouldn't be in it."

"We're fine. Nico likes it to be pampered *and* driven."

"I'm trying to do both."

He exited the interstate with expertise, taking a frontage road to the parking lot of his spiffy new building.

Cara looked across the empty lot where snow piles still clumped here and there. "This is your place?"

"Not my place," he corrected. "Castle's. The Electronic and Technology Castle."

Turning in the seat, she asked, "Did you name it that?"

"It's a nickname," he said, motioning toward the sleek glass front doors. "There's the real name. They did get the lettering up."

She took it all in. "Castle Technology." Underneath in smaller lettering, it read—*A division of Castle Department Store*, complete with the red castle-style logo.

"This is beautiful, Aidan."

He pulled up close, and then turned off the purring motor. "I can't believe it's really happening."

Cara's heart caved. He looked like a lost little boy who found a treasure chest, causing her to see him in a new light.

"This has always been your dream?"

"Pretty much. I wanted to work in this kind of store, but my mom insisted I run the electronics department at Big

Castle's."

"Did that have the same inventory?"

"No. We did a pretty good business, but we didn't carry a lot of the more advanced products. This store will have the latest devices, technology, digitally driven products. Everything electronic and state-of-the-art."

Cara enjoyed watching his face light up. "You've worked hard for this in the last few months."

"I want to make it work. Eleanor didn't have to give me this opportunity."

"Eleanor is a smart woman." Touching his arm, she said, "You will be great here, Aidan."

"How can you know that?" he asked.

"Because I know you."

His gentle gaze made her heart go wild. Every bit as attractive as his bad-boy-geek stares. "Do you want a private tour?"

"Of course." *When you say it like that, yes.*

They got out of the car, and Aidan hit the key fob to lock the vehicle. The store stood in a two-storied brilliance, all glass and chrome, the slanted roof reminding Cara of ship sails.

"Who designed the building?"

"An architect Eleanor recommended. I told her what I wanted and how I saw it in my head, then she worked her magic."

Cara stopped him at the doors to the lobby. "Wait? The architect was a woman? I'm thinking you did let her work her magic. Maybe even on you."

Aidan turned to give her a smirk. "Ah, are you jealous, Princess Fancy Pants?"

"I didn't say that. But rumor has it you like to love 'em and leave 'em."

"And look who's talking."

"Touché." He was right. "Okay, so I do the same thing. We really are a pair. Seems we avoid commitment like most people avoid the plague."

"But we're not a match."

Shocked and disappointed, she shook her head in a convincing denial. "No. That would be so wrong."

"We'd make each other miserable."

"Yes."

After he unlocked the doors, he opened one to allow her inside. Cara adjusted her leather coat and slouch hat. "Brrh. Hope the heat works."

"It will."

Trying to ignore how he'd adamantly explained away their attraction, Cara followed him through the aisles. Polished wooden floors held stark white and black rugs centered here and there. Listening stations for phones and test stations for electronic pads, laptops, and computers. Modern leather sofas and chairs in various colors that begged customers to relax and try out the merchandise. Chandeliers that looked stark and elegant, weighed by sturdy silver links. Stairs trimmed in wrought iron and gleaming steel. And mirrors everywhere.

Cara took him by the arm. "This looks like a wizard's headquarters. A good wizard. You."

"I'm no wizard," he said. "I know what I'm good at, and this is it."

"You're good at one other thing," Cara replied, her heart warm while her body shivered.

Aidan's dark eyes held her there. "And what's that?"

"The kissing theory," she replied. Then she kissed him to see if their attraction still worked inside this high-tech atmosphere.

It did.

Chapter Twelve

AIDAN PULLED AWAY to stare down at Cara. "We need to stop doing this."

Looking confused, she glanced around. "We just got here."

"The kissing—and you know that. Stop testing the theory."

"You're the one who came up with the theory. A good test by the way. I'm enjoying every minute of it."

"I don't think you're taking this seriously, Cara. You're on the rebound, big time. You got betrayed in the worst kind of way."

"You mean because a man wanted my money more than he wanted me? Yes, that's true. I got betrayed. Again. But this time, I wanted to be with that man, to marry him and have a family and live a life that would encompass my work and my world. I thought he was the one."

"Exactly." Aidan moved away to stand by an empty counter that would soon be filled with smartphones. Pressing his hands against the sharp angles of the glass, he shook his head. "This man really hurt you, and it's not just about the money. That's why you're acting out with me. Pure and simple."

Anger flared in her eyes along with another kind of hurt. "You think this is me acting out? What are we, Aidan? Fifteen? I don't go around kissing men to make my ego shine."

"Why do you and I do this then?" he asked, wanting to know the answer. "Why, Cara? I don't get it. We started out throwing barbs at each other … and then progressed to making out. I think we skipped a few steps in there. I've never done that with a woman before."

"I've never done that either," she said, her eyes full of remorse and aggravation. "I've tried to talk myself out of it a hundred times. I can't explain it."

Then she grabbed him by his jacket lapels, her face marred by a beautiful frown. "But I can assure you this is not acting out. This is acting *on*, Aidan. Acting on my feelings, on the way you make me crazy, or maybe because you do seem to regard me with such disdain and I'd like to change that."

"I don't disdain anything about you," he said. He covered her hands with his own, so he could gently remove them from his lapel. "I don't know what I feel right now. But I do like you. I didn't before, but I didn't know the real you before."

Cara pulled away from his hands, then folded her arms against her midsection. "You might like me, but you still think I'm flittering around without a care. But that is not true. Inside, I'm terrified—and not about Nico finding out or even about Trey taking the money."

She paced and held herself. "I'm terrified I've ruined the

one thing I do take seriously—helping people who truly need it. I do a good job with the Lamon Foundation. That I know. Other than seeing the monthly reports, my mother and brother leave me alone in that area. It's my personal life they tend to try to control."

"So you had this need to marry in secret to pull one over on them, and you failed."

"Yes," she said, her expression edged with pain and defiance. "When you grow up in a fashion house, you see a lot of drama. I've seen too many women obsessing about their wedding gowns, their men, and their marriages. So yes, I thought I'd pulled off the perfect wedding. No hassles, no interference, no talking me out of it, which usually happened long before I put a ring on it."

Throwing up her hands, she moved around the empty building, looking small and delicate against the high angles and sharp edges highlighting her in a shimmering spotlight. "I was wrong, so wrong, and now I might lose my job and my family's last shreds of respect. I could lose everything."

Aidan wished he hadn't pushed her. Meeting her mid-pace, he held her there, tugging her arms away from her body so he could be the one to wrap her in security. "I won't let that happen. I'll help you fix this. But … we can't pretend that you and me—that anything will come of this."

"I'm not pretending," she said on a husky note. "For the first time in my life, I am not pretending. That's the scary part." She whirled away, heading toward the chrome and wood stairs to the top level. "As Eleanor always says, we all wear masks and our lives are one big façade."

When she reached the stairs, she stepped up and twisted to look down at him with her famous haughty frown. "But the irony of this situation is that I've been more honest and real with you than I have ever been with anyone else. And you said you like the real me."

With that, she turned too quickly in her tall boots, slipped, and landed on her cute backside in a sitting position on the second step.

Tossing her hair, she said, "You can add graceful to my list of charms, too."

Aidan went to her. "Are you all right?"

"As usual, my pride is wounded."

He stood over her, trying not to laugh. But he couldn't help himself.

"Now you're the one not being serious. I could sue, you know."

"You wouldn't."

"No, I wouldn't." Her smile turned into a grin before she finally laughed, too. "Please tell me the surveillance cameras aren't operational yet."

"Oh, I might have to check and see. I'd love a copy."

"You wouldn't dare."

He helped her stand. "Can you feel your legs?"

"Yes."

"Any pain?"

"No, but I did hit my bum."

"Your cute bum."

"Stop flirting. You know where that leads, and you've made it perfectly clear we are to behave."

Now she'd gone all proper on him. "We have to behave. My head is spinning."

"Well, at least we're out of the house. Show me the rest of the place. After, we can find some dinner."

"Shouldn't you get back home and fuss over everyone in your Lady Bountiful beautiful way?"

"Is that how you see me?"

"I see a good heart and a beautiful person."

"Wow, I need to write that down."

Aidan shook his head. "You're a constant mystery."

"Says he who keeps thing so close to his heart."

"We *could* be friends," he offered. "I don't have many close friends."

"Me, either." She reached out a hand. "Shake on it."

"Kiss on it," he said, giving her a chaste peck on the cheek.

"I thought that was a no-no."

"That wasn't a real kiss. More of an air kiss."

"Oh, okay then."

He walked her up the open staircase, then lifted a hand to point. "My office will be up here—the one to the left with the glass wall facing out into the open area."

"So you can watch over your domain, of course."

"So I can watch over the Castle domain." He guided her past his spacious office. "I'll have a store manager who is good with retail and high tech, but he'll clear things through me. His office is next to mine. We have a break room across on the other side, and a few other offices here and there."

"And nice views," she said, taking in the many floor-to-ceiling windows that allowed for a tiny faraway peek of the Dallas/Fort Worth and Arlington skylines off in the distant with closer buildings and parks nearby.

"We hope to keep our employees happy."

"I'm sure they will be. When do you have your grand opening?"

"After Christmas. We couldn't get it finished in time, but we'll do a big push for Valentine's Day."

"And we will have all come full circle by then," she said. She made her way over to the windows, then stared out over the buildings and countryside. "But some of us could be starting all over again. But not in a good way."

Aidan tugged her close, giving in to the need to protect and hold her. "We'll figure this out, Cara. I won't let him hurt you ever again."

CARA SAT ON a red leather lounge chair and called to check on Marlena and Tobias, while Aidan talked to some of the workers who'd made it to the site.

"We're all a-okay," Tobias told her. "Marlena has her little house in order. I found some old furniture in the storage room in the barn, so we cleaned it up and put it in there for her. The sun is actually shining, and the snow is melting. The kids are happy, and her car has been fixed. I'll pick it up later. I can't thank you enough."

"Tobias, take a breath," she said, smiling through the glass at Aidan. He winked at her.

He'd been around Johnny Darrow too much lately. Johnny winked at Annabelle all the time. Now Aidan had winked at her. What did that mean?

"I'm glad you found the furniture," she told Tobias. "Mercy, we have all kinds of furnishings stuffed everywhere. I've talked to Marlena about helping out at the house, and I'll pay her a fair salary."

"She's willing to work. Loves that big kitchen. She can cook and clean like a dynamo."

"You don't have to convince me." Then Cara asked, "What about her husband?"

"That situation has been taken care," Tobias said, suddenly going tight-lipped and silent.

"Should I ask how?"

"No, ma'am, you should not."

"You didn't commit murder or anything like that?"

"No. But he will not come around and bother her again."

"What about the children, Tobias? I worry about the father coming back."

"He implied he wasn't the daddy type."

"That is really sad. My father, with his many flaws, was still the daddy type. But he never lifted a hand in anger."

"Then consider yourself blessed."

Cara said a silent prayer for Marlena, her children, and for the man who's tried to hurt the young mother. She prayed he never crossed paths with Tobias or his people again.

"Do we need anything while I'm out?"

"Nothing I can think of. You were due a day out. Aidan, too. And doing it together was a good idea."

"Well, that remains to be seen. But we're getting on a lot better now."

Cara wouldn't go into detail about how it hadn't been the best idea, but … something had shifted between Aidan and her after coming on this little outing. They'd gone from barbs and banter, then moved beyond the kissing theory to become friends who talked and laughed together.

He'd shown her every square inch of this two-story architectural wonder. They'd started building at this site even before the Lone Star store had been finished, so he'd had six months of nonstop planning and executing. His excitement was contagious.

She'd never felt this way with any other man. But could Aidan get past his own hurts to see they had something together? Was she just on the rebound and pushing things too fast? She didn't know, but her heart shouted to go for it.

She thought about his childhood. Aidan and Annabelle's father had loved them but lost them due to drink and Caron's manipulations. He'd died brokenhearted in another state, and they'd never been able to reconcile things with him.

Thankful Lila Lamon had made it a priority that her children would always be close to their father, she remembered how she and Nico spent summers here in Dallas with their mother and winters with their father, sometimes on Lake Como.

She'd have to take Aidan there one day.

Snapping out of that projection into the future, she got back to Tobias. "We'll probably have dinner in town before heading home later."

"I'll leave a light on for you."

"Thank you, Tobias. And you're right. I am blessed."

"Me, too, suga'."

After ending the call, Cara checked on Aidan. Still in discussions, but he smiled and nodded his head at something one of the construction foreman said to him.

Deciding to check the Lamon Foundation newsletter, she skimmed the articles her staff put out every week regarding updates and new developments. She'd signed off on this one before she'd left … for her wedding.

Moving right along over new ventures and celebrations with the many people they'd helped, she spotted words that shook her to her core.

Where in the world is Cara Lamon?

Her hands shaking, Cara read the short article, dread filling her soul.

Our fearless leader seems to have dropped off the face of the earth. Could she be globetrotting in Bali or maybe on her way to the States to attend her brother Nico's much-touted wedding to Eleanor Castle in Texas? Why is she hiding out?

And then:

More later, if we can find her. If you see her, snap a picture and tell her we miss her!

Shocked, Cara glanced around and into Aidan's eyes. He must have sensed her apprehension. Holding up a finger to the two men in his office, he hurried toward the closed glass door and came out to where she sat on the lounge.

"Cara, what's wrong?"

She handed him the phone. "Read this."

He skimmed the article. "Did you approve this?"

"No," she said, getting up to pace. "No. That's much too vague and flippant for a professional newsletter, and it wasn't in the proof I signed off on. What will people think?"

Aidan pushed at his bangs, gripping his hair while he studied the article. "Find out who might have written and approved this. If it didn't come from your staff, it could mean Trey hacked into your website, copied the original, and added this post before it went out."

"He's sending me a message, isn't he?"

"Yes, if he did this, I'd say he's sending you a strong message. One that shouts loud and clear that he knows exactly what we're trying to do. We might not know where he is, but he wants us to understand that he knows exactly where *you* are."

Chapter Thirteen

THEY ATE A light dinner at a neighborhood café, but Cara wasn't hungry. "This has turned serious," she said, knowing it sounded lame and weak. "I thought he'd go away with the money he already had."

Aidan played with the condensation on his water glass, catching the tiny beads with his finger. "He's not going away without the rest of the money. He'll do whatever it takes to flush you out."

"I thought we were flushing *him* out."

"We are and because women are starting to respond, he's becoming desperate. But his is a smart kind of desperate."

"He'll be bolder next time, too."

"Yes." Aidan leaned toward her. "Cara, whatever you do, don't go to my fake media sites, okay? He can trace you from there. He knows you're in Texas, but he won't get near you if I can help it."

When they were in the car and on the way home, the last little bit of sunshine tiptoed over the tree line. "Aidan, I have to leave."

"What?"

"I have to go back to Milan and take care of this mess."

"But it's days until the wedding. You can't leave and go

back there. He might not even be there, or he might be setting you up so you'll go back. The word is out on him, so he's getting desperate."

"He will find me. Here," she said, knowing she shouldn't have run in the first place. "I have to face this head-on. I've been hiding out like a ninny, thinking it would all go away."

"I can make it go away while getting justice for you," he said. "I need proof." Shooting her a questioning glance, he added, "I cleaned up any trace of you being with the man but if he's as sharp as he seems to be, I'm sure he's got some evidence of his own."

"You mean to make me look bad?"

"Yes."

"I haven't done anything unethical. I wouldn't do that. I have comptrollers in place to watch out for discrepancies."

"He can hack right into your bookkeeping accounts, Cara."

Cara felt the panic overtaking her. Trey could go far back into her life and do damage. Fidgeting, she said, "I need to go back. I have to go back."

Aidan did a quick turn off the main road and hit the brakes, causing the Jag to skid and come to a halt in a small park area.

"What are you doing?" she asked, her hands on the dashboard.

"Trying to talk some sense into you. You don't have to go back to Italy. But if you do go back, I'm going with you."

"What about your store? What about the wedding?"

"The store is on track, and the people I have in place

know I travel a lot. And I'll have you back by the wedding, I promise."

"We'll draw him out. I'll make him come to me."

"No, he'll see that as a trap. Too dangerous."

"Not if you're there with me."

Aidan shook his head. "Only if we have people in place to nab him before he can hurt you."

"Yes, we'll have the authorities with us." Relaxing a little, she added, "With what you've found on him and with my people gathering evidence and protecting my money, we should have a solid case. But even if we can't prove anything, at least we can convince him it's over. He won't get any more Lamon money from me."

"Cara, promise me you'll be careful. He could turn dangerous."

"I'm aware of that. I hope some of his other victims will speak up, too."

"That's already happening on my fake online profile. I'm sure that's what has him in an uproar."

Cara sent Aidan a grateful smile. "So we're doing this?"

He lifted her hand, his fingers entwined with hers. "But we do all of this on one condition."

"What's that?"

"You have to tell your family what we're doing, in case something goes wrong."

"Aidan…"

"I mean it. I never reported my suspicions about my mother, and I never confronted her. If I had, I might have been able to head things off before Eleanor got involved. I could have forced her to turn herself in—quietly and without all the press and gossipmongers watching."

"Do you think we can make Trey do that—come quietly?"

"No, but I don't care about Trey the way I cared about my mother. And I sure don't care about him the way I care about you."

Staring out at the blinking car lights up on the freeway, she nodded. "I shouldn't involve you, Aidan. But I'm so glad you're willing to do this for me."

"I'll want a reward," he replied, his eyes coal black in the gloaming.

What kind of game was he playing? "A reward? I'm not sure I understand."

"We can practice that kissing theory a little more," he said. "Once we're free and clear and can really trust each other." Then he cranked the car and let the motor purr, while her heart purred along with it.

Another kind of panic overtook Cara. Trust was such a delicate thing, and she wasn't sure he trusted her completely. "I fear that kissing theory is going to get me in a lot of trouble," she retorted. "But you have a deal."

"Good." He had the Jag back on the road and flying before she could catch her breath. "We'll go home and make arrangements."

Cara took another breath, then said, "Oh, no. We can't do that. We can't go to Milan."

"I thought we'd discussed this."

"My mother is coming. She could be there when we get

home."

"So we tell her the truth. If she doesn't approve, we'll have to explain how important this is."

"It's my career," she said. "I did everything by the books with Trey, just as I would have with any foundation money changing hands. I might seem flaky and impulsive, but I take my job very seriously. We have a lot of checks and balances, and it all appeared legitimate—to everyone."

Aidan watched the road, silent for a few moments. "If you explain to Lila and she agrees and approves, I won't force you to tell Nico. Yet."

"Okay. I think that's the only way to handle it because it's not just about the wedding and ruining it. If we tell Nico, my brother will want to rush in with guns blazing and save the day."

"And you want to save the day on your own, right?"

"Right," she replied. "But with a little help from a friend."

An hour later, Aidan pulled the Jaguar into the garage and pointed to another car parked inside. "Did your mother rent a car at the airport?"

"What?" Glancing up from jotting notes on her phone, she gasped. "That's not my mother's car. That's the sedan Nico and Eleanor bought a couple of months ago. They keep it at the estate."

"Do you think?"

"I don't know but … I've got to get inside and find out who else has decided to show up at this ranch."

"DARLING, YOU HAVE some explaining to do."

Cara air-kissed her mother, relishing the scent of gardenia and jasmine in the perfume her mother wore. *Lila.* Created for her by the man who loved her but left her, Cara's father Leo.

Standing inside the big room where the Christmas tree shined like a beacon, Cara shot a glance over her mother's shoulder to Aidan. Did she know already?

"What do you mean?" she asked Lila.

Dressed in winter white wool from head to toe, Lila looked as elegant as always. Nothing ruffled her feathers. But this might.

"I come home to find an adorable woman cooking up a storm in my kitchen and two delightful children reading books near the tree." Lila gave her a bittersweet smile. "It reminded me of you and Nico when you were young, and things were … different."

Letting out a sigh of relief, Cara laughed and waved a hand in the air. "You've met Marlena and her children then."

"Yes, and heard the whole explanation from Marlena and Tobias, but I couldn't help teasing you a little bit." Lila took Cara's hand before smiling at Aidan. "Hello, Aidan, nice to see you again."

"Good to see you, too, Mrs. Lamon," he said, back to being quiet, studious Aidan.

Cara could only imagine what was going through his

mind. He'd needed peace, yet he'd had nothing but chaos.

"Call me Lila," her mother responded before giving Cara a pointed glance. "Cara, I'm so proud of you for helping Marlena and her family. Tobias is beside himself but so thankful."

"Mother, you know I had no other choice," Cara replied, standing back to glance down the hallway. "Did someone come with you?"

Then she heard heavy footsteps coming from the kitchen.

"Yes, someone did come with her."

Nico Lamon stood there, dapper in jeans, a navy sweater, and handmade Italian boots, his inky-black hair falling around his temple and his deep blue eyes on Cara. "And someone still has some explaining to do."

Whirling toward him, Lila shook her head. "Nico, we just got here, and Cara and Aidan just got home. Let them settle in and then we can talk."

"I only wanted to know why my car was missing from the garage, Mother," he said with a wink. Stepping forward, he shook Aidan's hand. "I can tell you haven't had much privacy staying here. That's how things tend to go at the ranch. And whenever my sister is involved."

Aidan lowered his head and grinned. "Never a dull moment." Then he shot Cara a glance that held questions and concerns.

Cara smarted underneath Nico's smug words. Why did her infuriating brother make her feel as if she were still ten years old? Would she ever get out from under his big shadow?

"I've tried to stay out of Aidan's way," she said in her defense. "I've been busy myself. Wedding things and getting everyone settled around the ranch."

"She's right," Aidan added. "I've hardly noticed her being here."

But the look he gave her told Cara he was very aware of her. Saving face with her big brother.

"No matter. We're *all* here now," Nico said. "I dropped Eleanor off at the estate. My bride is working on last-minute details. I never knew how much goes into planning a wedding."

Lila chuckled. "Well, soon it will all be worth it. Until then, we can relax by this beautiful tree and remember what this season is all about."

"Great idea," Nico said, his dark gaze settling on Cara. "I can't wait to catch up."

But Cara knew her brother. He'd heard something. She saw the slight disapproval in his frown. He'd be polite in front of Aidan, but he'd corner her later.

She might be forced to spill everything to Nico after all.

And if she knew her brother, he'd never allow her to go back to Italy to confront her con artist ex-fiancé.

AIDAN LOOKED UP at a rap on the office door. Nico stood there, two glasses in his hands.

"So how are things with the new store? Eleanor's received

your reports, and she's very pleased."

Aidan took the shot of amber-colored whiskey Nico handed him. "A little off schedule due to the weather, but the crew has worked double time the last couple of days to get back on track. That's where Cara and I were earlier."

"And did my industrious sister give you decorating advice?"

Aidan shook his head, swirling the whiskey around in the crystal glass. "No. She complimented me, but ... she didn't make any suggestions."

"She has a lot on her mind," Nico replied before taking a sip of his drink.

Aidan waited a beat. "Yes."

"This wedding has all of us on high alert. Cara is a very private person, but she has her social butterfly moments. I was surprised she'd arrived here early."

"You and me both," Aidan admitted.

"Exactly how did she arrive here?"

Ah, now they were getting down to the nitty-gritty.

He wouldn't lie, but he wouldn't divulge either. "I came home late one night and found her ... on the couch in the den."

"I see. Odd that she didn't let us know."

"I didn't ask questions, Nico." *Not too many anyway.* "After all, the house belongs to all of you. I'm the interloper here, and I properly should head back to the estate."

"You are welcome here, and you have to stay for my bachelor party." Nico's amused eyes brightened. "So you're not intruding, but I'm sure my sister insisted you were."

"She did, but we worked out a deal of sorts."

Nico finished off his drink. "I'm sure you did."

Aidan sat quietly, his method of making people talk.

But Nico didn't talk. And Aidan couldn't read the man. The fire crackled, and the room creaked.

While they had a stare-down that reminded Aidan of two gunfighters waiting to pull the trigger.

Nico got up, then placed his empty glass on a nearby tray. "I trust you, Aidan. Remember that."

Without another word, he left the room, leaving Aidan in the dark with a glass of whiskey to console him while he wondered who *he* could trust.

Chapter Fourteen

CARA PACED IN her room. Marlena had walked back to her cabin. After greetings, explanations, and updates, Tobias had gone home, too.

Then her mother had given her that Lila stare. "Something is wrong, and you need to tell me what it is."

Cara had planned to tell her mother the truth, but now Lila would immediately bring her brother in on things. "What do you mean, Mother? Everything is on schedule for the wedding."

"I'm not concerned about the wedding. It will be what it will be. I'm concerned about you. You left early for that trip to Bali, which I thought odd considering the wedding, and now you arrived here before us and didn't even tell us. I know you don't like us snooping in your life, but honestly, Cara, your actions seem off-kilter to me."

"I didn't go to Bali," Cara admitted. "Change of plans. A work thing I had to deal with."

"Is that why you seem so jittery? Or is it Aidan?"

"Aidan? Why would he make me jittery?"

"Do you really think I haven't noticed?" her mother asked, a hand that sparkled with jewels touching Cara's arm while Lila held her little lap dog Gigi close.

"Mother, don't make anything of me being here with Aidan. He was here when I arrived, then we got snowed in, and now he'll stay for the planned bachelor party. You and I will go to Eleanor's bachelorette party in town."

She should blurt out the truth, but Nico being here had thrown that plan out the window.

"Of course, darlin'," Lila said with an elegant eye roll. "Cara, I wasn't born yesterday. I know a flirtation when I see one."

"No one is flirting, I can assure you. We barely tolerate each other."

"But you two were certainly together when you came in the door looking as guilty as a dog with a gnawed-up shoe."

Not liking that comparison, Cara laughed. "My guilt came from moving people into our home without clearing it, but I knew you'd understand. I hope so at least."

"Hmm," Lila said, giving Gigi a wink. "We'll let it ride right there, but … I'm watching you two."

Like a hawk, too. And so was Nico.

Cara had managed to extract herself on the pretense of powdering her nose, which neither of them probably believed.

Her mother and brother were downstairs in the den, quietly talking. How could she tell her mother the truth with Nico here? He was obviously curious about why Cara and Aidan were together today.

And where was Aidan?

A knock at her bedroom door caused her to jump.

She really needed to stop pretending to be deep into international espionage. Because she didn't have the nerves for such charades.

Hurrying to the door, she asked, "Who is it?"

"Aidan."

Swinging the door back, she tugged him in and shut the door behind him, locking it to be sure.

"Do you think that's a good idea?" he asked, motioning to the locked door.

"Do you have a better idea? As in, what do we do now?"

"That's why I'm here," Aidan said, his onyx eyes moving over the room. "Nice digs, Princess."

"Have a seat." She motioned to the dainty blue chaise lounge by the window.

Aidan stared at it as if it were a foreign object, but he sat down on the edge of the chaise and immediately looked way too masculine for this room.

"What do you want?" she asked, irritation at her predicament front and center on her mind.

"We have two choices," Aidan said. "We can sneak away to Milan and let everyone think we're an item, or we can stay here and tell your brother and mother the truth and let them know what we plan before we leave."

"Are there any other choices?"

Aidan lowered his head and stared at her underneath that shadow of bangs, causing her heart to skip and leap toward running away to Italy with him, consequences or not.

"There might be one more option," he said, his voice low and husky.

"I'm waiting."

"We stay put and stay quiet."

Cara sank down on the edge of her bed. "What? That's even more dangerous. Trey could get away."

"We've done everything possible to contain this and to flush out Trey. That's working. My anonymous social media sites are on fire with women who remember him under numerous aliases, and they all agree he's a lying scumbag who bilked them out of money. That kind of defamation will make him mad. Extremely mad."

"And we do nothing?"

"We wait," Aidan replied. "He'll come here sooner or later. All I have to do is tell the authorities—"

"No, Aidan. That's too risky."

"We can't bring him down on our own. That would be even more dangerous."

"I don't mind confronting Trey," she said, welcoming that meeting. "But I won't put my family or you in danger."

"So you'd rather risk going to Italy to face him? Italy, where the authorities don't play around and where your home and organization are located, where so many people depend on you?"

"Why wouldn't I? That's where this all started."

"If we contain it and draw him out, make him to come to us, we can probably end this very quietly, once and for all."

"You never wanted me to go back anyway," she pointed out.

"No, I didn't." Reaching for her hand, he said, "I'm worried if you go back there, even if I'm with you or nearby watching out for you, that he'll do or say something to convince you to forgive him."

"You think I'm that weak?"

"No, Cara, I think you're still in love with the man."

Cara let go of his hand, wondering how he could possibly think that when she and Aidan tested the stupid kissing theory over and over and proved *they* were attracted to each other.

Was he in denial?

Was she in denial about Trey and Aidan both?

Aidan took her silence for admission. "You do still care about him, don't you? Is that why you need to go back? Because you want him to love you and you need to hear that from him?"

She stood and started pacing. "You are so off base, Aidan."

"Then why aren't you telling me no, that you don't love him?"

"Is this about the scandal we're trying to contain or is this about us?"

"Us?"

"Don't look so perplexed," she snapped. "You know there's something brewing with us."

"Like storms all around?"

"Yes, like that, but only when we're alone together." Stopping, she whirled to face him. "I never told you this but after we kissed at the costume ball, I began to doubt my love for Trey. I got confused and my rock-solid plans to elope in a romantic, defiant way shifted to me wondering if I'd made a huge mistake."

"Well, at least you came to your senses, but I think you already had doubts and that's why you kissed me. You used to me make or dispute a point."

"No, that's not true."

"Then why did you kiss *me*, Cara? I'm sure any number of men at that event would have been happy to help you figure things out."

Gritting her teeth, she looked into his eyes. "Because I wanted to, okay? I wanted to kiss you, Aidan. Blame it on the champagne and Toby Keith."

"Toby Keith?"

"That song and you, looking all bad-boy in that gambler getup. How could I ignore all of that?"

His expression changed from moody to triumphant as he stood and moved toward her. "I'm not sure I like being used that way, but … I did enjoy it." Leaning close, his face inches from hers, he said, "I don't play second fiddle, and I don't do rebound romance. I might act like a gambler at times, but not with my heart, Cara. And not with you. We are not rushing into another disaster, understand?"

Cara took his stipulations in, wishing his words didn't sting so much. "Well, then, why are you so keen on going to Milan with me?"

"I'm not keen on it," he replied, still too close. "But I won't let you go alone, and that's final."

"You don't have the final say in this."

"Yes, I do. I've put myself on the line to help you."

"I'm going, somehow," she stated. "With or without

you."

Aidan's phone dinged rudely, forcing them apart.

Cara thought about grabbing her purse and getting in the Jag to make a run for the airport, but Aidan managed to move himself in front of the door.

"Yes. I understand," he said into the phone. "Thanks for the report." After he ended the call, he leaned back against the door to give Cara a stern once-over. "We're not going anywhere."

"I told you—"

"We can't go to Milan, Cara. Trey Wellington is not there. He's in New York at that fancy apartment he told you about."

CARA SHOOK HER head, trying to absorb this new development. She'd never believed Trey would dare come to America. "Trey is in the States?"

"In New York City," Aidan repeated. "And I'm thinking he'll be on the move again soon. He'll hop a plane to Dallas. Just in time for your brother's wedding."

"I should have stayed there and murdered him," she said with a fierce sincerity. "That would have taken care of all of this."

"I'd have to come and visit you in jail," Aidan pointed out. "I wouldn't like that."

"I'll probably wind up there, anyway."

"You didn't do anything wrong."

"But I might if he shows up here."

"Let him show up," Aidan said. "Same plan, different time zone. We can draw him out and surround him with police officers. If for no other reason than him threatening or harassing you."

"And how will we do that with my brother sitting downstairs?"

"He'll be busy with wedding stuff."

"He'll have on his golden radar."

"He's already onto us, I think," Aidan said. "I'm not sure what he knows, but he knows something."

"I think my mother does, too. Did you say anything?"

"No, of course not. But he tested me with a shot of really good whiskey."

"That's so like my brother, trying to get you drunk."

"I can hold my liquor, and I can hold off your brother."

"But you don't like doing that."

"No, I don't. But hey, I fell on my knees and pledged my alliance to you the night you showed up in that white dress and," he bent down beside the chair and picked up her bridal pumps, "these shoes."

Cara glanced over her shoulder before turning back to him. "If I had a sword, I'd knight you on the spot." Tugging him close, she said, "You're my dark knight. No matter what."

Aidan dropped the shoes to take her into his arms. "And you're my Princess Fancy Pants. Or maybe I should change that to my runaway princess bride."

After seeing her wedding shoes in his big hand, she made

a decision she knew she'd regret. "Let's go downstairs and spill our guts to the king, my knight."

"Are you sure?"

"Yes, I'm sure. Because I believe no matter what, you're my only protector right now."

"No matter what," he said, sealing their bond.

She only hoped she wouldn't live to regret her declaration and the promise they'd made to each other.

Chapter Fifteen

LILA AND NICO sat silent and stern across the dining table
from them. Lila glanced at her son and then back to her
daughter.

Then her gaze pinned Aidan to his chair. "Thank you,
Aidan," she said, her tone calm and soft.

Before Aidan could respond, Nico let out a sigh. "Yes,
thank you for helping Cara with this situation. But we all
know this man will show up here sooner or later."

"I won't let this ruin your wedding," Cara said, her voice
strong now. "Aidan kept advising me to tell you both the
truth. Now I'm doing that, so we can stop Trey before he
tries to create a scene."

Aidan watched Nico's face for signs of his anger. But
Cara's brother seemed to be just as calm as her formidable
mother.

Nico got up to pour himself more coffee. Cup in hand,
he leaned against the counter. "Cara, did you truly believe I
wouldn't hear about this?"

"Yes, I thought I could take care of it and have it done
before you arrived here."

Nico shook his head, giving her a soft smile. "Cara, I
knew all of this before I arrived here."

"What?"

Both she and Aidan sat up straight.

"How did you know?" Cara asked, shock making her skin turn pale. Then she shot Aidan a glare. "Did you tell him?"

Aidan felt the stab of her distrust all the way to his bones. Looking her in the eyes, he asked, "What do you think?"

Cara stood, then started clearing away the uneaten pie her mother had placed by her coffee cup. "I don't know who to believe anymore. Everyone around me lies to me—for my own good."

Aidan wasn't going to defend himself against that. He hadn't lied to anyone. He'd only tried to protect her, and she wanted to turn the tables on him in front of her family? So much for being her knight and protector.

Nico finished his coffee, then put his cup in the sink. "Stop it, Cara. Aidan didn't alert me to anything. But I have a right to know about transactions that have to do with the House of Lamon."

Still in a rage, she said, "But I'm in charge of the foundation. We've discussed this before."

"Yes, and you do a good job. But that doesn't mean I don't keep tabs on the finances. What kind of CEO would I be if I didn't?"

"What exactly do you know?" Aidan asked, figuring it was open season now.

"I know my sister was dating a mysterious man she'd planned a trip to Bali with," Nico replied. "I also know she transferred funds from our main bank to another bank where accounts are harder to trace. Which meant this had to be foundation money or my sister was trying to hide something. Turns out you were hiding a lot of things."

"How could you know that?" Cara asked, holding onto the high back of her chair. "You've never once questioned me or compared notes with me. I thought you trusted me."

"I do trust you, but I have to take care of our business, all of our business," Nico admitted, a hand moving through his dark hair. "I trusted you, Cara. You've done a great job, and you've found your niche." Shrugging, he said, "I had no reason to mess with that. Until now."

"But you're doing it all over again," she said. "Hovering, watching, waiting."

"Not waiting, Cara," Lila said. "He's not waiting for you to fail if that's what you think. Your brother is doing what he's been doing since Leo died. He's protecting the Lamon legacy."

Nico sat back down. "I didn't know about the wedding. I had my doubts about Trey Wellington, but I let the lawyers and investigators take care of that. He checked out, so I didn't interfere."

Lila shook her head. "Honey, why would you hide your wedding from us?"

Cara glanced at Aidan, her expression full of a mortified regret. "Because of this—the need to always watch out for me, check up on me, and scare away anyone who tried to have a relationship with me. I wanted to keep Trey to myself because he seemed so perfect."

Turning away, she said, "But he wasn't perfect and now,

even though I went through the proper procedures regarding the foundation money I authorized for him, I've still made a mess of this and … to think you knew most of it the whole time. I'm sure that's why you're both here early, right? To check on me and let me know I'm not as independent and self-sufficient as I thought."

"Cara…."

She whirled to face her brother. "No, Nico. No, don't tell me this was for my own good. I've heard that one too many times already. I'm going to take care of this, and I don't need any of you to help me."

With that, she turned and ran out of the room.

Aidan heard the back door slamming.

"I'll go after her," he said. Then he stood face to face with Nico. "She's good at what she does, and she has a big heart. I can promise you this, Nico. If I find Trey Wellington, he will never hurt her or any other woman again."

Grabbing his jacket, he hurried after Cara, not caring what her brother or mother might think. Not caring about his high-stakes technology store or even how Eleanor would feel.

He only cared about Cara, even if she didn't truly believe in him.

Now he understood both sides of this equation.

Nico loved his sister, and he wanted to protect her.

Cara loved her brother, and she wanted to make him proud.

The clash of the Titans.

And Aidan was caught slap in the middle.

But he went to *her*. He knew now he'd always go to her. No matter what.

CARA WRAPPED THE shawl she'd grabbed at the back door around her like a security blanket, the cold December wind shoving at her with a brutal assault. She headed to the bench she'd sat on a few days ago wearing a wedding gown and those ridiculously high-heeled white shoes, her heart broken, her faith in humanity shattered.

Aidan had saved her in more ways than one. Yet in her need to prove everyone wrong, she'd lashed out at him. Her knight in shining chrome and heavy metal, his castle cast in sharp glass and shimmering light.

"What have I done?" she wondered out loud. The wind lifted her words, bringing back a whirling chill but no answers.

Then a soft warmth surrounded her. Aidan and his suede button-up coat. He tugged her with him into the warmth of that big coat and held her close, kissing the top of her head.

"I didn't rat you out, Princess."

Cara turned and buried her face against the flannel of his shirt, inhaling that clean, crisp scent that made her think of snow and ice and fire and warmth. He was all of those things.

"I know," she said. "I know. I'm so sorry I doubted you."

"Don't doubt me again."

She lifted her head, tears cold against her cheeks. "I

won't. Ever."

He kissed her, his arms holding her against him, the warmth of his security bracing her against the chilly night. She'd come here broken and afraid because of a man who'd let her down, and found a man who not only measured up to her standards, but also kept her on her toes and challenged her in so many ways she wanted more. She wanted him.

Aidan lifted his lips from hers. "You have to believe this, Cara. I wouldn't be in this if I didn't believe I can help you and keep you safe."

She bobbed her head, wanting his lips back on her. "I know. Trust is a hard thing to comprehend, but … I think that's why I kissed you that first time, Aidan. I trusted you from the beginning. I didn't know that until tonight."

"So the kissing theory works?"

"The kissing theory proved to me that I should have gone with my instincts. I shouldn't have gone back to Italy to marry Trey. I won't make that mistake again."

"I won't let you make that mistake again," Aidan said on a growl of a whisper. "You're with me now, got it?"

"Got it."

She touched her mouth to his. "Sealed with a thousand kisses." Then she lifted and pushed at her windblown hair. "Trey can't hurt me anymore. I hope he does come here. When he does, I'll be ready."

"And I'll be there with you."

"So what next? We wait to hear from him?"

Aidan wiped a tear off her cheek. "First, we go back inside where it's warm, and … then we check on Trey the

Betrayer. A friend in New York has been watching his apartment, and we've hacked in on his electronic devices. If he sneezes, I'll know about it."

When she tried to stand, Aidan tugged her into his arms, his eyes moving over her face. "I'm making sure you don't run away again, princess."

Cara felt light in his arms. She could walk but why? He'd lifted her up like a Viking about to take charge. "So I'm at your mercy now?"

"Yes."

Cara didn't argue with him until they got to the back door. "What about Mother and Nico?"

"What about them? You're with me now, remember?"

"Okay, that works."

Leaning her head against his solid chest, she breathed a sigh of utter relief and joy. Maybe this would all be okay after all. At least Aidan made her feel that way.

Then she felt panic again. "Nico will want to take over and stop this, Aidan. He'll send out his goons."

"I have goons of my own."

"That won't matter."

"I'll explain things to your brother."

Cara giggled. "And I'll buy tickets to that."

"Okay." He shoved the door open. Still carrying her, he called out to her surprised family. "I found Cara. We're going to finish what we started by bringing Trey Wellington to justice. We'd appreciate it if you don't interfere unless we ask you to do so, understand?"

Lila nodded, her eyes wide. "Clearly."

Nico grunted, his eyes blazing with fire. "This is ridiculous—"

"Nico," his mother said, her tone brooking no argument. "Leave it."

Nico studied them before shrugging. "Fine. I just want to marry Eleanor and go on my honeymoon, anyway."

Aidan's held her brother's thunderous gaze and matched it. "I've promised Cara. She's strong and she thought she had to do this alone, but … she's with me now. We're going to clean this up, so we'll never have to talk about Trey Wellington again."

Nico's expression shifted from enraged and confused to accepting and grateful. "All right then."

Aidan gave them a curt nod. After carrying Cara into the office, he slammed the door shut.

AFTER HE PUT her down, Cara clapped her hands and hugged him close. "I've never seen anyone stand up to Nico that way before."

"I can't believe I did it," Aidan admitted. "But if he interferes now, he could mess this all up."

Touching her hand to his face, she gazed into Aidan's eyes. "Thank you for standing by me."

He pulled away. "I need to check to see if Wellington's made any sudden moves."

Why had he pulled away? Had that little scene with her brother been for show? Did Aidan truly care about her or

LENORA WORTH

was he just puffing up to impress her brother?

She'd been so sure moments ago, but her doubts made this dark room even more sinister.

"Princess," Aidan said, motioning her over. "He boarded a flight out of New York about an hour ago."

"He's coming to Dallas, right?"

Aidan nodded. "He'll arrive sometime overnight."

"It's on," Cara said, focusing on what might come next.

"It's on," Aidan echoed. "I need you to stay alert and … don't do anything stupid, okay?"

"You think I'm stupid."

"No, I think you're brave, but a bit reckless and impulsive."

"Well, that sounds so much better."

He touched her cheek. "I need you to stay safe. We have a lot of days ahead of us to get to know each other without worrying about this hanging over our heads, okay?"

Well, that sounded like a commitment.

"All right. I'll be alert and practical."

"You'll call me if something develops while we're apart?"

"Yes."

And once this fiasco was over, she'd find out how Aidan really felt about her. He'd told her not to doubt him, and she wanted to believe she could depend on him.

But neither of them could make a commitment until this mess was behind them. Then they'd have to decide if their growing feelings were real or part of some sort of grand charade.

Chapter Sixteen

AIDAN STOOD WITH Nico, Tobias, Johnny, Claude, and Saul out by the sprawling white barn. A cold wind whipped across the pasture, but they had a fire pit going and big steaks on the grill. The barn was equipped with an open-air kitchen and a fancy sound system that blasted twangy country songs.

He thought about the first time he'd kissed Cara, with Toby Keith's song warning him not to kiss her like that.

He wanted to kiss her like that even more now. Not sure what had happened to him, Aidan decided he might be up the creek without a paddle. But it was too late to grab a rope and save himself.

"Whose idea was it to have a cookout in December?" Johnny asked, lifting the collar of his wool peacoat to cover his ears.

"Same person who planned a December wedding at the downtown park," Nico said with a grin. "Eleanor thinks she can control heaven and the earth."

"Doesn't she?" Aidan asked, wondering what Cara and her mother were doing right now.

Nico laughed at that. "Sometimes I think she has a lot of connections in high places." He pointed to the sky. "She's convinced that second round of predicted winter storms won't interfere with our wedding."

"If anyone can hold off a snowstorm, it's Eleanor," Claude said, raising his glass.

They all toasted Eleanor.

Now that the roads were clear, the women were supposed to leave for town so they could enjoy Eleanor's bachelorette party at the estate while the men did whatever men were supposed to do at bachelor parties.

Nico had wanted this one low-key and on the ranch, which suited Eleanor fine since she wanted the same with her pre-wedding party at the estate since her father had rooms on the other side of the house and she didn't want to disturb him.

They were trying to keep the wedding intimate by inviting only a small group of coworkers and family. But the local media had already reported this weekend's events, so Aidan expected news trucks and helicopters at the Dallas Arboretum. He almost wished another storm would show up, so they'd have to move things inside at least.

Aidan wanted to find a corner and go into his own world, but those days were over. He'd have to leave Texas to find any peace this week.

Marlena and the children were in their little house, warm and safe. After the wedding, Marlena would take up her new position as housekeeper and assistant to Tobias. She glowed with gratitude. Lila hummed along, cooing at everyone and smiling with a mother-of-the-groom kind of happiness.

But he worried about Cara. She'd seemed on edge since

hearing Trey was in New York and then on his way to Texas.

This morning, he'd barely had a chance to speak with her, but they'd eyed each other with unspoken words. Lila had ordered everyone to take their places to prepare for the wedding on Saturday.

"This wedding isn't going to happen if we don't all get moving," Cara's mother had stated at breakfast. "Men here and women at the Castle estate. We have a busy couple of days. The parties tonight, the rehearsal dinner tomorrow night, and then the wedding Saturday at sunset. A chilly sunset."

Cara had trailed after Lila, both talking at once. Wedding excitement had taken over.

Aidan longed for those first few quiet weeks he'd had here after the Lone Star Castle store had opened with a record turnout. All summer and most of the fall, he'd stayed hard at work on his own store, trying to avoid the spotlight while his sister relished it.

Now, it was his turn. By February, he'd be cutting the ribbon on the Castle Technology grand opening. But no gimmicks. No designer shoes involved and no costume balls to attend. Just a sleek black-and-white grand opening cocktail party for some very important people—his new staff and the whole Castle clan of workers, including Eleanor and Nico, Johnny and Annabelle, and the rest of his close family and friends.

And maybe he'd have Cara by his side.

"What are you musing about?" Tobias asked from his place at the grill. "Did your morning milk go sour?"

Aidan glanced around. Claude from the big store was talking to Saul from the Lone Star store. Nico followed the conversation, interjecting a few words here and there. Johnny stood apart, listening and laughing while he held his cell phone to his ear.

Aidan turned back to Tobias. "I'm thinking ahead. I have a busy schedule once the wedding is over."

"I aim to sleep once this shindig is over," Tobias said. "That and Marlena showing up have both tuckered me out. Happy doings can be as bad on the ticker as big shoot-outs."

"I hear that," Aidan replied, lifting his beer. His heart had come alive and beeped at him several times over the last few days.

Johnny moseyed over, a big grin on his face. "Your sister is fit to be tied."

"What now?" Annabelle, the drama queen.

"She's angry you didn't tell her Cara was here with you."

"Annabelle heard Cara talking to me the other night when I was on the phone with her. I thought she'd figure it out on her own."

"She didn't. Too caught up in wedding mania." Johnny put his hands in the pockets of his coat. "Now she's planning *your* wedding."

"My wedding?" Aidan shook his head. "Way too soon for that."

"I never dreamed I'd be getting hooked in the spring," Johnny said, his eyes holding so many conclusions. "So never say never, my friend."

Aidan lowered his head to stare at his boots. "I didn't say

never, just not so sure right now."

Nico walked up and stared them both down. "I never thought I'd be standing here at my own bachelor party, especially not with you two." Slapping Aidan on the back with a little too much emphasis, he added, "But … we're all family now. Bonded together by Castle Department Store."

"And some interesting, smart women," Johnny pointed out.

"I think that place put a spell on all of us," Aidan admitted. "Things tend to happen like magic around there."

They all directed their gazes to Claude and Saul, now standing with Tobias.

"The three Musketeers all look mighty proud of themselves," Johnny said. "I do believe Claude is the real Santa Claus. He's made a lot of kids happy during this Christmas season. They flock to him, and don't even cry."

"And Saul is one of his elves."

Nico lifted his eyebrows. "Tobias is like a western wizard, all cowboy poetry and sage advice."

"Maybe they're all leprechauns," Johnny said on a low whisper.

"We can hear y'all," Claude called out with a chuckle.

Johnny shrugged and waved back. "I've been good, Santa. Remember that."

"You're right," Nico replied. "They have conspired to make us fall in love." He sent Aidan that Nico look—part warning, part acceptance.

Was Aidan in love with Cara?

Johnny and Nico both seemed to be waiting for him to

respond, but he wasn't sure how to frame his feelings.

The back door opened and feminine chatters escaped, saving Aidan from the awkward silence.

Cara rushed up to him, dragging him away from her brother's overly interested glare. "We're leaving."

"I can see that."

"Any news?"

"Yes. Your boy is in a boutique hotel in Dallas, and he's found a bank."

Her face went blank, but not before Aidan saw the apprehension. "Are you afraid of Trey?"

"No," she said, scoffing. "I'm afraid of what he might try to do, but he never threatened me in any way."

Aidan's gut told him she might still have a few secrets, but he couldn't confront her again. She either trusted him or she didn't. Still, he worried.

"But he's coming after you, Cara. People become dangerous when they need something desperately or when they've got nothing to lose. Remember that."

"Maybe he's found a new woman to finance his dreams," she said on a flippant note.

"He's not done with you, but we'll catch him before he strikes again."

"I'll see you tomorrow night at the rehearsal dinner," Cara said, her anxiety gone now, her eyes telling him she'd like to kiss him goodbye.

"I'll be there, unless something happens."

"What could possibly happen?" Lila asked as she came by.

Cara held up her hand. "Oh, nothing, Mother. Storms, traffic, the unpredictable things in life."

Lila's vivid eyes moved between them. "Sometimes, the unpredictable things are what makes life exciting."

She moved on, her perfume leaving a floral trail in the wind.

"Does she know something?" Aidan asked Cara.

"She knows everything, she thinks."

"I need to stop staring at your lips all the time. Your brother is giving me not-so-subtle warnings to stay away from you."

"Did he threaten you?" Cara asked, spinning toward her brother. Nico gave her a sheepish smile. His signal he still loved her and would protect her in his older brother way.

Aidan tugged her back around. "Not in so many words. He says he trusts me."

"And I trust you. So we're all good to go, right?"

He wanted to believe that, yes.

"Right. Have fun with the girls. And by the way, Annabelle knows about us."

Letting out a tiny gasp, Cara said, "Oh, my. She'll unleash on me like a Texas tornado."

"Just warning you."

"Okay. You have fun with the boys."

"I'll see you tomorrow night." He looked into her eyes. "The estate has good security, and we've posted guards."

"Yes, Nico told me. If you hear anything…"

"I'll let you know." He added, "And I'll come find you."

Cara believed him. He'd bring a whole army with him,

too.

So she left him, safe in the knowledge he would be there to help her if she needed him.

And … she did need him. In more ways than one.

ENGULFED IN CHATTER the minute she entered the Castle estate, Cara tried to take in the scope of the place. Having been here only once while too keyed-up about kissing Aidan the night before, she'd missed the beauty of the rambling Tudor-style mansion. Eleanor had done a major overhaul, lighting things and adding new furnishing and art to complete the beauty and turn it into a modern, livable home. She redone a set of suites on the lower level to accommodate her father and a full-time nurse, too. Her father's dementia didn't allow for many visitors, but Eleanor sat with him and talked to him every night.

Cara stood admiring the house until Annabelle grabbed her in a death grip. "You should have called me."

"Obviously, since you seem to have missed me so much," Cara replied, trying to extract herself from Annabelle and all of that long black hair. "Let go of me before I suffocate."

"Does your mother know?"

"She thinks she knows, but I've neither confirmed nor denied. It's complicated."

"Tell me," Annabelle replied, her hot pink tunic long and sleek over black tights and tall boots. "Eleanor and I want all the details."

"I don't think your brother is ready for me," Cara admitted. "But I'll share what happened this week."

Not everything, of course. She couldn't share the sordid details of her botched elopement. Too embarrassing. Besides, this was Eleanor's time to shine.

And shine she did in a white cashmere sweater, a gold dangling necklace, and skinny jeans that had sparkling gold stars embroidered on them to match her shimmering gold ankle boots—a Lamon classic.

"Cara, welcome," Eleanor said, beaming a bride's smile. "And Lila with Gigi." She hugged Lila, then took the wiggling white dog and air-kissed Gigi while the dog barked approval.

"It's so nice to see you again," Cara told Eleanor.

"I hear we have a lot to talk about," Eleanor said, her blonde hair falling around her shoulders. "Tiffany is on her way. Meantime, we have food. Fajitas and margaritas or mojitos. We also have wine and cheese, Castle Cookies, and all sorts of munchies. I have to watch what I eat, however. I have to fit into that dress."

"Can't wait to see it," Lila said, smiling. "Nico is so ready to see *you* in *it*. And still pouting that he's not allowed to see the final version."

Eleanor got that dreamy look she'd had since she'd met Nico. Cara loved her brother but truly, Eleanor was so in love with him and he loved her right back. While he drove Cara nuts at times, she couldn't help but to be happy for him. Maybe he'd back off from overshadowing her life once he got married and settled. She thought of Aidan, then allowed her heart to go ahead and lurch into a little dance.

Was she in love with him?

Annabelle's dark eyes met hers. "So, Cara, how do you feel about my brother?"

Eleanor and her mother stopped chattering to stare at her.

"I don't know," she admitted, her gaze moving over the other women. "But this is Eleanor's party, and I don't want the emphasis to be on me. Let's go sit by the fire, and then we can swap tales."

Lila sent her a comforting glance and a nod. "We might as well wait for Tiffany. She'll want to hear everything about this latest romance."

Romance. That sweet, comforting word surrounded Cara, causing her to get all dreamy like Eleanor "I suppose so. Not much to tell, but … we never know, do we?"

"I think I know," Annabelle said. "I knew the first time you two met each other."

The doorbell rang, saving Cara from blurting out what her heart had known from the beginning.

She cared deeply for Aidan.

She might even be in love with the man.

Chapter Seventeen

CARA CAME DOWNSTAIRS the next morning to find her mother puttering around the huge kitchen. "You're up early, Mother," she said, giving Lila a kiss and lifting Gigi to give her a doggie smooch.

"I'm too excited to sleep," Lila said, her silvery bob falling into perfect symmetry. "My son has found a woman to match him in every way, and now my daughter seems to have fallen in love, too."

Cara pulled her soft robe against her matching pajamas. "I shouldn't have gone on and on about Aidan last night."

"We all wanted to hear," Lila said, her gray eyes full of pride and worry. "But you left out the part about Trey Wellington."

Last night, she'd explained how she'd arrived at the ranch early. And explained everything after that. In the meantime, she and Aidan connected on many levels.

"Especially with Marlena and her children."

Annabelle had listened with awe-filled silence. "It's the children," she said. "I remember our mother holding us close and telling us it would be all right. Aidan knows how those children felt. And now, he knows your true heart."

And all of her friends and family knew she might be falling for Aidan. Things could change so quickly, Cara wasn't sure what would happen next. She had the added worry of waiting for Trey to show up.

"I deliberately left out the sordid details regarding Trey. Thank you for not mentioning him," Cara replied after her mother handed her a cup of coffee. "It's too humiliating."

"Humiliation. That's why most scam victims never come forward," Lila said, rubbing her hand across Cara's shoulder. "But you, my darling, are a Lamon, and you also come from strong Texas stock on my side of the family. We will fight this, Cara."

"No, I'll fight it. Alone," Cara retorted.

"Not alone, exactly," Lila reminded her. "You have a new crusader now."

"Aidan," she said, wondering about his true character.

Lila kissed her on the cheek. "I believe you can trust him, Cara. He's a good man."

Cara had to remember that. She needed to trust Aidan.

If she couldn't trust him, she'd be doomed forever and never fall in love again. The man had come to her defense last night in a way she'd never forget.

Sipping her coffee, she stood staring at the vast backyard. Winter had settled over Dallas like a dark cloak, but the Castle gardens looked well-maintained and beautiful in a stark, untethered way. Old camellia bushes bloomed in soft pinks and dark fuchsias. The ancient oak trees out beyond the pool mushroomed up to the sky, their undergrowth full of azaleas that would bloom next spring. Garden paths lined with benches and rock formations meandered down to a small creek. Even in the cold, this place breathed warmth and tranquility.

Peaceful and lovely. She'd have to go for a stroll to clear her head.

But the kitchen filled up with women. Soon, they were eating Lila's Mediterranean vegetable and feta omelets and munching on fresh croissants and fruit.

"I had a lovely time last night," Eleanor declared, lifting her mimosa glass. "I'm blessed to have all of you in my life."

She glanced around at each of them, then took a good look at her home. "For a long, long time I stayed out there on my own, afraid, depressed, full of rage and vengeance. Then I came back, determined to take back what I had lost. I'm not proud of how I went about it. Annabelle, I'm so sorry I had to bring your mother to justice. But ... I promise when she is out of prison, I will do my best to forgive her."

Annabelle nodded, her eyes misting. "You've more than made up for what happened. I'm happy now and in love with Johnny, and ... I think Aidan is on his way to a better place. Even Caron should be glad about that." Doing a classic Annabelle eye roll, she added, "At least she's speaking to us again. I think she's secretly proud of us both for carrying on."

"I hope so," Eleanor said. Then she turned to Cara. "And you—I know I'm going to enjoy having you for a sister-in-law."

"A double sister-in-law if she hitches up with Aidan," Tiffany said, her chuckles sounding like wind chimes, her dark eyes bright with hope.

Cara held up her hand. "Not so fast. Aidan and I are …
trying to figure each other out. Please don't mention our
conversation or what I told you last night to him." She
glanced at Annabelle. "We all know Aidan will bolt if I push
too hard. I don't want him to bolt. And I'm notorious for
doing the same, so I have to think my way through this."

"True." Eleanor smiled at Cara. "We'll keep your secrets."

Then she went on to thank Lila and to pay tribute to her
best friend, Tiffany. "You've been a constant in my life since
we were teenagers. I'm so happy to have you as my matron of
honor."

"Oh, it's real. It's happening," Tiffany said, beaming her
brilliant smile. "I can't believe this fairy-tale wedding will
take place tomorrow afternoon."

Lila held up her phone. "And possibly during another ice
storm."

The radar showed storms moving from the northwest.

"No," came the collective protests.

"It can't snow again," Eleanor said, getting up to check
the weather outside. Clouds had already formed. Then she
let out a sigh. "Well, if it does, we'll make this work. I want
to marry the man I love and if I have to stand in the snow,
then so be it."

Lila stood, too. "Then it's settled. This wedding is on, no
matter what."

Cara remembered the promise she and Aidan had made
to each other. *No matter what.*

Maybe that was the answer to love. No matter what,

people had to make it work and when they really loved someone, they would make it work.

Much later when they finished going over the final plans for tonight's dinner here at the estate, her phone buzzed.

Thinking it must be Aidan since he'd texted her earlier to check on her, she hurried upstairs to her room so she could get dressed after she talked to him. The caterer had already arrived, and the dining table and other tables brought into the big central hallway had been decorated in beautiful burgundy and cream to match the holiday decorations and the massive Christmas tree in the formal living room.

But the unknown number wasn't Aidan.

"Hello," she said, knowing the voice she'd hear.

"Cara, you weren't that hard to track down. So predictable."

"Trey, I wondered when you'd show up since you knew I'd be here anyway. But you wasted a trip. You need to understand I'm done with you."

"Not so fast," he said. "You left me in such a hurry. I thought if we could talk…"

Cara didn't want to sound anxious to see him. "I have nothing to say to you. Why don't you cut your losses before I call the authorities?"

"And tell them what? That you gave me money for my cause and we were secretly engaged? We both know you do not want a scandal, especially on the all-important weekend of your brother's wedding."

That sounded like a threat. "What do *you* want?"

"I'd like to meet with you. Talk this through. I do love

you."

"You're ridiculous," she said, anger coloring each word. "You don't know the meaning of love. Unless it involves money, of course."

"I do love you, Cara. I broke my own rule and fell for you."

Thinking she should meet with him and get this over with, as she and Aidan had planned, Cara started to remember everything Trey had done—making her fall in love, convincing her to fund his fake cause, taking her money, and having the nerve to show up wanting the rest of it. But anger and bitterness changed her mind. She didn't care anymore. Her mother and Nico knew everything already, and they still loved her. Aidan knew it all, and he still fought for her. The people who counted would understand and forgive her.

"I don't think that's a good idea." Cara swallowed the bile rising in her throat. "I have to go. Do what you think you need to do. I'd rather go through a scandal than deal with you."

"You don't know what you're talking about," Trey replied. "Your man Aidan Castle has been messing where he shouldn't be."

Cara's heart did a spin of fear. He wouldn't go after Aidan, would he? "I don't believe you."

"You should listen to me. You really don't know him, do you?"

"I have to go."

"He's a low-level hacker, Cara. Has been for years."

Cara wanted to cover her ears and end the call. But she

didn't. Aidan was brilliant, but Trey made him sound like a juvenile criminal.

Trey took her fear and ran with it, working it to his advantage. He went on, his voice calm. "He hacked into your accounts and your private files, and he has a dossier on you. He thinks we're in this together."

"That's not true." Aidan had questioned her over and over, and she'd assured him she had done nothing wrong.

"He won't admit it, but it's true. I can prove it to you."

Cara closed her eyes. She wouldn't believe this man's lies.

And yet, a little niggle in the back of her mind wondered if Aidan hadn't played her, stringing her along to get information on not just Trey, but on her, too. Had he planned to expose them both in order to look good in Nico and Eleanor's eyes?

What if he'd done that? What if he'd never trusted her, and he'd just been bidding his time? She didn't have anything to hide, but it would still hurt.

Then Trey dropped a bombshell on her.

"You might want to consider this. I set up a dummy account with some of the money you *loaned* me—the Lamon Foundation's money. It's under your name since you inadvertently signed off on it. If he finds that account, you'll look guilty of embezzlement."

"That can't be true. I'd never sign off on anything like that."

"You did, sweetheart. I bundled it with some of the wedding papers, then had you sign them at dinner one night. You signed off on the venue I picked and our honeymoon accommodations, remember? I have the money free and clear, so I put it in a special place. It can easily be traced."

His laughter grated across her nerves like jagged wires.

"You told me once, Cara, about how you'd siphoned money in your younger days. Remember that?"

Her Robin Hood account. No one knew about that.

"I didn't take foundation money," she said, thinking her past sins had come back to haunt her. "I was young, and I wanted to get even with my father for breaking my mother's heart. I played with the bookkeeping and hid some funds, but you know what I did with most of that money."

"Right. You have a heart for charity cases, so you gave some of it to employees who'd been fired or laid off. Such a Lady Bountiful. Do you think your brother and your board of directors will find that amusing?"

A teenager acting out but in a big way. Soon after that, her father had died and Nico had taken over. But she'd kept that secret stash. Just in case the Lamons or any of their employees needed it.

Could she ever find true security?

She'd told Trey that in confidence after he'd shared some of the details of his troubled upbringing. But as Aidan had said, Trey would use whatever he could against her. Once she'd come back from college and Nico suggested she take over the foundation, Cara had never touched that money. Had practically forgotten about it.

For a rainy day, as her mother always said. Cara had taken that to heart, but … her brother had no idea.

Cara's stomach roiled with dread. She'd gleefully signed

some papers. Anything to marry the man of her dreams. But she'd never dreamed he'd hunt down her secret account and use it against her. And create more accounts to make her look bad.

Surprised he hadn't cleared out the account, she swallowed her fear and dread. "You are even more evil than I realized, Trey."

"I think you're beginning to see things my way," Trey said. "I'd like us to meet tomorrow at noon." He named the Reunion Tower. "Fitting for a reunion, don't you think?"

"Why do you want to meet with me?" she asked, her head spinning with nightmare images. "You have the money. Take it and go. Take my secret stash, too. We'll call it even."

"I want the rest of it," he said. "And I need you to help me get it. Since we're not married, I have to have you with me and you know that."

"So what are you going to do? Force me to go to Milan with you?"

"Yes. I have your fake passport ready, and I have a plane waiting." Pausing, he let out a long breath. "This is about so much more than money, Cara. If I can't have you, no one will."

"I won't go anywhere with you."

"I know what you're thinking. You'll tell everyone at the rehearsal dinner that I'm harassing you. I'd advise against that. I know where the Castle estate is located. I might show up for tonight's rehearsal dinner, just to give a thorough update on the intimate details of our relationship. I haven't made up my mind."

"If you show up here, you'll be taken down, Trey. Nico won't let you get away with this. Neither will Aidan."

"I'm not worried. Aidan has some explaining to do. Nico will want to protect the precious Lamon name. But he'll be in foul mood for the nuptials."

"You can't possibly think your threats will work."

"If you don't do this, your embezzlement will hit the media at about the same time your big, bad brother is walking down the aisle. He'll have the press waiting for him outside the church. A pity he'll have to cancel his honeymoon. It's your choice, darling. Keep quiet tonight and put on that brilliant smile, then meet me tomorrow. We'll make this quick and easy."

What other choice did she have? "I'll be there." But she wasn't getting on a plane with him. She'd figure a way out. Somehow.

But then he added one more stipulation. "And Cara, please come alone. If you bring anyone, or announce this to any law enforcement personnel, I'll drop a few more dummy accounts into the clouds and I'll report Aidan Castle as the hacker he is. You'll both be arrested at your brother's reception. The head of the Lamon Foundation sited for embezzlement and off-shore accounts, and the man in charge of the state-of-the-art technology store a low-life hacker. How's that for a headline?"

She sank down on a chair, staring blankly out at the old oaks. "I'll be there. Alone."

"That's my girl."

Cara ended the call. She was not his girl. But she had to

get to Aidan and let him know she'd heard from Trey, and she needed to explain about that hidden account. He might have already found it. Which meant she'd never be *Aidan's* girl, either.

Chapter Eighteen

AIDAN STARED AT the figures on his computer screen. Lamon Foundation money hidden away in a private account, just as his investigator had said. And under Cara Lamon's name at that. Not a large amount, but significant enough to look suspicious.

Blinking, he remembered carrying her into the office and telling her she was with him now. But did she want to be with him? She had no reason to hide money, but the transfer appeared legitimate.

Why hadn't she put this money into her holding account in Italy?

Maybe she didn't do this.

Logic told him not to believe the documents. That Trey had managed to breach her accounts, or that he'd somehow used money she'd given him to set this up to make her look bad.

But then his friend Paul had hinted that Cara might be hiding money. Or at least that was what Trey wanted people to think.

Paul had reminded him again. "It's called the Robin Hood account for a reason."

What was that reason? Did she steal from her family to

give the money to the poor? Or to men who wanted money? Had she been trying to buy love? Or could she be just as criminal as Wellington and Caron?

Aidan checked his watch. He had to leave for the rehearsal at the venue in the park and then dinner at the estate. He'd try to catch Cara alone to ask her about this. Trey had to be involved.

But Cara's signature was there. How had Trey gotten it?

A knock on the door to the small bedroom he'd moved into last night made him shut his laptop. "Coming."

Nico stood there, dressed in a dark suit, his hair combed in place and a nervous energy radiating around him. "Ready?"

"Yes." Aidan grabbed his own suit jacket, then checked his burgundy plaid tie. "Think I'll pass muster?"

"I was going to ask you the same," Nico replied. "And I wanted to talk to you privately."

"Sure." Aidan shut the door and turned to stare at Cara's brother, seeing the resemblance now that he'd been around her for a week. "What is it, Nico?"

"I know I'm not supposed to worry about Cara and this latest crisis, but I need your assurance that she's safe and you both know what you're doing."

Aidan thought about the documents he'd seen. "She's safe. I texted her earlier. As you know, we have guards at the Castle estate to keep the press away."

"And to protect my family," Nico said. "I don't want the wedding ruined—for Eleanor's sake if nothing else, but I do care if anyone in my family gets hurt or worse."

"I feel the same. Trey Wellington is in Dallas, and I have people watching him. He's going to try to make a move on Cara, but I'll make sure that doesn't happen."

"Does Cara know that?"

"She knows he's here and that I have people watching him. But neither of us knows what he'll try next."

Nico did a neck roll, clearly tense. "Do I want to know how you've managed to stay on top of this?"

"Better that you don't," Aidan replied. "I haven't done anything illegal. Yet."

Nico nodded. "And … do you also have people watching *her*?"

Aidan thought about the thumb drive containing everything Paul had sent him. "For now, no. The guards at the estate have been alerted, and I've given them photos of Wellington. He won't be able to get on the estate grounds."

"Should we put a man on Cara?"

"You don't trust your sister?"

"Do you?"

"I'm trying to, yes. I promised her I'd stand by her."

Nico looked perplexed. "But?"

"But we have rehearsal and then dinner. They're all riding together from the estate, except for Tiffany. Her husband Jasper is bringing her. I'll be there with Cara at both places."

"I suggest you don't let her out of your sight," Nico replied. "I love her, but I also know her. Cara can be impetuous when she sets her mind on something."

"And her mind is on getting Trey out of her life."

"Yes. She might try to slip away to take care of this on

her own."

"I won't let that happen," Aidan said, meaning it.

"I take that to mean you do care for her then?"

Aidan could admit that. "I do. Does that concern you?"

"No, no." Nico's chuckle went brittle. "Now that I've accepted this new development, it makes me smile. You two going nose to nose... That will be fun to watch."

Aidan wasn't so sure about that. Before he and Cara could move to the next level, they had to clear up this one little matter of getting her ex-fiancé out of her life— preferably behind bars. If that was what she truly wanted.

"We'd better head out," he said, too many whirling thoughts clouding his head.

Nico followed him out the door. Johnny and Saul were meeting them at the park. Claude had agreed to give Eleanor away since her father wasn't able to attend the wedding, and said he'd find his own way. Tobias had declined attending tonight's festivities, so he could stay on the ranch with Marlena and her kids. They were going to have a special pre-Christmas dinner in her little cabin before the big Christmas gathering on Sunday. That left Aidan riding with Nico in the Jaguar.

Which only made Aidan remember driving the sleek automobile with Cara by his side. When he got in on the passenger's side, he smelled her unique scent—flowers and something undefinable. Vanilla maybe?

Today and tomorrow, then the wedding would be done. But what would Trey do? Show up at the rehearsal dinner? Crash the wedding? Or would he do something more devious and sly, such as waiting patiently and then exposing what could look like embezzlement to the world? Cara's embezzlement.

Aidan prayed he hadn't fallen for a woman who might be just like dear old Mom.

No, Cara was not like Caron, even if their names were similar. Cara had a heart, and she cared about people. This had to be a setup. Why couldn't he see that, free and clear?

HER NERVES WERE quivering and jangled. She had to talk to Aidan. But what if he did go with her and something happened to him? He'd been watching Trey like a hawk, so he'd probably trace him to the Reunion Tower anyway.

No, she had to warn Aidan to stay away. She'd done enough damage by ignoring her problems. Time to make things right by facing Trey head-on herself.

"What's wrong with you?" Tiffany asked from behind Cara.

She tensed and took a breath, pasting on a smile before turning toward her. "Nerves. Weddings. Stuff."

Tiffany wore her lush braids curled around her head like twisted black ropes. Her gold earring dangled against the sleek print of her burgundy and black full-skirted dress. She wore Lamon kitten pumps.

Her keen gaze pinned Cara to the spot. "Is it Aidan?"

Cara glanced around the spacious room where they were all meeting before heading to do a walk-through of the wedding ceremony in the garden. Decked out for Christmas, with a fire burning, this place was the perfect backdrop for a romantic holiday wedding. Outside, the chilly early evening air battled with a determined sun, but soon the sunset would hit the water where the white pelicans frolicked in warmer weather.

"Cara?"

"Yes, and no," she admitted to Tiffany. "I'm confused and joyful and scared and hopeful."

Tiffany nodded, her lacquered fingernails touching on Cara's black wool coat. "Well, honey, pick one and stick to it because your man is on his way over here."

Tiffany did a fast getaway to the other side of the room where Eleanor stood talking to the minister.

Cara pulled herself together before facing Aidan.

He wore a suit that could work only on his body. Black and bold, tailored and slim cut, his plaid tie festive against his white shirt, his dark bangs covering those amazing, unreadable eyes. She wanted to run to him and confess all.

But ... she didn't know where to begin.

"Hi," he said, his gaze dancing down her body. She'd chosen a silvery cocktail dress that flared out at her knees and silver Lamon shooties—part boot and part shoe—to finish off her outfit. His gaze indicated he'd noticed.

"Hi," she replied, her heart burning. "You clean up nicely."

"So do you, princess."

They stood staring at each other. Silent.

"Are you okay?" she asked, wondering, worrying.

"I'm good. How about you?"

"I'm anxious to get this done. It's chilly out there."

"Yeah, me too."

"You're anxious?"

"I'm ready for some downtime. Too many weddings."

Noting his distant stare and unyielding expression, Cara tried one more time to get through the walls he'd put up. Did their brief time apart make him rethink the kissing theory and her being with him now?

She reached up to touch his cheek. "We could run away. Somewhere warm, safe, and quiet. No weddings and no scandals."

He touched her hand, his fingers moving over hers, his eyes as dark as a moonless night. "We could."

Silence again, his gaze holding hers, asking her questions she couldn't answer.

And then her mother's voice, calling out. "Everyone's here. Time to rehearse the ceremony."

The moment ended, and Cara tugged her hand away.

"We need to talk later," Aidan said, a whisper just for her.

"Yes. Later."

She had to tell him the truth. If she didn't, she'd lose him if she tried to go after Trey on her own.

But she might have already lost Aidan.

She couldn't tell what he was feeling.

That scared her more than facing Trey Wellington.

AIDAN STUDIED HER after they arrived back at the Castle estate. She was nervous, jittery, her eyes darting here and there. At the rehearsal, she'd shivered and studied White Rock Lake, oblivious to the sparkling white lights on the trees and the gazebo-inspired exhibits along the paths of The Twelve Days of Christmas, something Eleanor wanted her guests to view as they proceeded to the wedding venue.

They'd made it through the rehearsal with a brilliant sunset and the wind dying down. But inside, Aidan churned and burned. Especially when he had stood with Nico, Cara across from him with a smile pasted on her face. Tomorrow, he'd escort her past all the guest once the wedding was over.

What then?

But sometime between now and then, he'd have to ask her the tough questions. They didn't need any more surprises or secret between them.

He found his chance after the formal dinner when all the thank-you gifts had been handed out and the toasts had been made. Eleanor and Nico were happy, but Nico had shot both Aidan and Cara a couple of concerned stares. Aidan hated to mess with their happiness. Eleanor looked pretty in her cream dress and matching shoes. Since she didn't have a clue about this little scandal, all was right in her world. Annabelle looked smitten, hugging onto Johnny, her Goth days over even if she still managed to look edgy in a bright red fitted dress and red patent boots. She only thought Cara and he were playing a game of who would cave and fall in love first. Aidan had already fallen. But he wasn't sure about the woman he'd fallen for.

But he did know he only had eyes for Cara.

So he slipped up beside her as she stared out at the sparkling lights in the garden. "Walk with me."

"It's cold out there."

"I'll go get your coat."

She nodded, her expression tight and guarded when he returned and helped her slip her coat over her dress.

They went out through the French doors to the massive porch and patio. The outdoor fireplace sizzled and hissed, its warmth spreading into the night. Beyond the porch, the pool sparkled with floating white lights in bright red poinsettia-inspired containers. The whole yard twinkled with tiny white lights spread across the shrubbery and trees.

"I love this garden," she said, wrapping a white scarf around her neck. "I've wanted to take a stroll since I arrived back here yesterday. I'm glad I waited, so we can see it together. It's magical."

"You've talked to Trey, haven't you?"

Her body tensed, straightened, until she stared up at him. "No."

Disappointment hit Aidan in his gut. "You do know I've been monitoring his phone calls, right?"

"And have you been monitoring mine?" she asked, indignation sparking in her eyes.

"What if I have? You asked me to help."

Her expression changed to regret. "I didn't ask you to spy on *me* or to dig into my past."

"He told you I was?"

"He told me a lot of interesting things."

"Who do you trust, Cara? Him or me?"

Holding her coat together, she lowered her head. "I don't know, Aidan." Then she reached for him. "No, I take that back. I trust you. I have to trust you."

Aidan knew her heart, but he wanted to hear the words from her lips. "Then why didn't you tell me the truth?"

Chapter Nineteen

CARA'S WORLD BEGAN to crash around her. "I wanted to tell you, Aidan." She glanced up at the house, all aglow in candlelight and sparkling lights. A winter wonderland.

"But you still don't believe that I mean what I say."

"I've had doubts. But, apparently, so do you."

"What did he tell you?"

"That you're not only harassing him, but also gathering information on me."

He didn't deny it.

"I guess Trey's telling the truth on something at least."

"I can't very well gather information on him without checking on you, too, Cara. I have your cell phone and computer records on a thumb drive."

"And my bank accounts?"

He stared off into the distance. "I have a financial investigator friend who did some digging."

"On both Trey and me?"

"The two go hand-in-hand."

"And let me guess. Your investigator found my Robin Hood account."

Aidan whipped his head back around, his eyes burning dark. "Yes. And I'd really like to know about that account …

and why you failed to mention it since it could be considered embezzled money."

"Embezzled? That's what Trey wants everyone to believe. He's played both of us, Aidan."

"Maybe, because you believe him over me."

"He said you're a hacker."

"I am a hacker, but … that's because I know how hackers work. I learned a lot in tech school, and I learned a lot in life. This thing with you—this is the first time I've ever pushed the envelope. To save you. To help you."

"And to find possible discriminating evidence on me," she retorted, her heart breaking. "I set up that account years ago with money I'd earned working at the House of Lamon, Aidan. I got angry when my parents divorced, and I went to a young man in accounting who had a major crush on me. It didn't take much to convince him to syphon off money to help some of the workers who'd gotten laid off when things got so bad. I was eighteen and full of self-righteous anger, so I made sure those people got the funds they needed."

"Why do you still have the account? Because now Trey is calling it embezzlement."

She looked down, ashamed and frustrated. "I went off to college and left it alone. I couldn't tell Nico, so I kept the account … for a rainy day. I know it's silly, but … I never felt secure after my parents split up."

"And money brings you security?"

"No, Aidan. Love brings me security. But I've never really had it because every man I've met wants my money more than he wants me. Trey was the last straw."

"Not every man, princess," he said, his hand touching her cheek. "You're with me now. No matter what, remember?"

"How can I be with you if you don't trust me?"

"I could ask you the same."

"So what now? Are we done? Over?"

"We have to beat Trey at his own game."

"No. I have to beat him."

"You can't do this alone, Cara."

"I'm not," she said, hating to lie to him. But she wouldn't risk him going to jail on her behalf either. "I told Trey to take the money, even my Robin Hood money. He has access to some dummy accounts and that account. He can walk away with close to half a million dollars."

"And he agreed to that?"

"Yes."

"I don't believe you."

"You never did."

With that, she turned and went back inside, shivering. But not from the cold. Her body trembled with the need to turn and run to Aidan. Let him take care of this.

She'd done that early on. Because of that, he might be in trouble, too. Her only hope lay in meeting with Trey to convince him to cut his losses. Or go back to Milan to end this once and for all. But she'd only agree to that if he left Aidan alone. She had investigators, too. She could build a case and expose Trey, but not until after her brother was happily married and she knew Aidan was safe.

AIDAN LEFT THE party and headed back to the ranch, his heart burning with the sure knowledge that Cara had lied to him.

He'd found her phone when he went to get her coat from the hallway closet. And because he had to know, he'd checked the numbers on her recent calls. Nothing much except an unknown number with a Dallas area code.

Trey. It had to be him. A burner, of course, but all of her other calls had identified the callers. This number stood out. They'd talked about five minutes. This afternoon.

That explained why she'd been so jittery all night.

She'd admitted she'd talked to Trey, and she didn't want Aidan to protect her.

Exactly like when her brother tried to protect her.

She'd meet with Trey, but what would she do? Run away with him and forgive all? Take her bank account funds and head to Bali? Marry the man?

Or sacrifice herself to save face for her brother and for Aidan?

He wouldn't let her do that.

So he called in reinforcements. "Johnny, I need you, Saul, and Claude to help me with something. Tobias will be in on it, too. But you can't tell anyone."

He quickly explained the situation in generic terms.

"I'm in," Johnny replied without asking who, what, where, or how. But he did ask, "When do you need us?"

"I'm not sure. Could be anytime tomorrow or could be

during the wedding."

"Ah, right. How do you plan to explain this to Eleanor and Nico?"

"I hope it won't come to that. Just be on standby, and let's hope this is all cleared up before the wedding."

"You got it," Johnny said. "Hey, is this legal—what you need?"

"Yes. Some surveillance and protective detail stuff."

"Okay, man."

Then Aidan called Annabelle.

"What? Do you know how late it is?"

"I need your help," he said, not bothering with apologies.

"What's wrong?"

"I think Cara might bolt sometime tomorrow or maybe during the night even."

"I'm not staying up all night to watch your girl, Aidan."

"You won't need to," he said, turning his Jeep around to head back to the estate. "I'll do that. But I can't be at the estate tomorrow. You have to let me know if she leaves alone."

"Okay … you know she's notorious for running away from relationships, obviously."

"Yeah, I know that. But she's with me now."

"Aidan, you can't force her to love you."

"She does love me. She just doesn't know that yet."

Annabelle let out a purring chuckle. "This is gonna be epic."

"Watch out for her."

"I will. I like Cara. Let's try to keep her around."

Aidan aimed to do that. Keep her.

He wouldn't let her noble heart take a hit for the team.

She was part of the team.

CARA HAD NOT slept well. She'd paced around the spacious room Eleanor had assigned her, staring out at the lights in the back garden. Once, she could have sworn she'd seen Aidan standing down in the shadows, but she'd blinked and he'd disappeared. Wistful thinking, nothing more.

Now, bleary-eyed and in need of coffee, she practically sleepwalked into the kitchen to find Eleanor sitting at the counter, crying.

Panic roiled through her stomach.

"Eleanor, what's wrong?"

Eleanor tugged at her robe and wiped her eyes, her golden hair cascading over her shoulders. "I went in to see my father."

"Is he all right?"

Eleanor bobbed her head. "I told him I was getting married today, and that I wished so much he could be there."

Cara put her arm around Eleanor's shoulder. "I'm so sorry. It must be hard when he doesn't recognize you or understand you."

Eleanor raised her head, her eyes glistening. "But he did know me. He smiled at me and said, 'Eleanor, you will make a beautiful bride. Just like your mother.'"

Cara teared up. "What a wonderful gift."

Eleanor nodded. "Yes. Amazing. I have to call Nico."

Cara watched her hurry off. After pouring a cup of coffee, she thought about being with Aidan out in the garden last night. That might turn out to be their last moments together.

"I should have told him that I love him," she whispered.

Too late, she could see that Nico's hovering only meant he cared about her, and that Aidan's digging into her past had been inevitable if he wanted the truth. He'd gone out on a limb for her because he cared about her family. And her.

She turned and went back upstairs to prepare for the day ahead, dread weighing heavily against her heart. She'd finally found a man who could love her, and she'd managed to lose him because she hadn't told him about how she'd acted out in the past. What she hadn't told him was she'd added money to the Robin Hood account—money she'd earned fair and square. But that didn't matter now. She'd ruined everything.

AIDAN WENT ABOUT his day, talking with Nico, monitoring the weather, checking his phone, and wondering how he'd ever get through this wedding. He'd done Cara one last service, a nearly impossible feat he'd managed only because he had her phone files downloaded and readily available.

"Snow predictions for later this afternoon," Tobias said when he'd stopped by for coffee. "But I'm guessing everything is still a go."

He gave Aidan a defiant stare. Aidan nodded. "Yes, the wedding will take place."

Tobias knew what else might be taking place, too.

At around eleven, Aidan got a text from Annabelle.

She's gone. Disappeared. Called a car service. Left a note that she'd see us at Castle's to get dressed.

Aidan texted back. *THX.*

He'd put a GPS on every car in the Castle garage.

Cara had called for a ride, so no way to track her vehicle.

But he'd also put a tracking app on her phone.

Pulling it up, he stared at the screen. She was heading into downtown Dallas. He texted Johnny. *It's time to move.*

Then he went to find Nico.

"I'm going into town early. Some business I need to take care of."

Suspicion washed over Nico's face. "What's going on, Aidan?"

Aidan clapped a hand to his shoulder. "Best you don't know. Focus on your bride and don't worry. We'll all be the wedding."

"I don't like the sound of that."

"Now if only my Jeep will crank."

Nico nodded toward the garage. "Take the Jaguar. I'm driving my sedan today."

"Are you sure?"

"I think I am," Nico said, his blue eyes full of questions. "Aidan, keep her safe, please."

"That's why I'm heading out now."

Nico called after him. "What about your tux?"

"Bring it with you," Aidan said, hurrying away.

Soon, he had the Jaguar growling at top speed while he zipped in and out of traffic, all while directing his ragtag army on where to go and what to do.

"She hired a car to take her to the Reunion Tower."

"I'm on it," Johnny said. "And everyone is with me."

Aidan breathed a sigh. "Tobias is right behind me, too."

"You are seriously going to a lot of trouble for this woman," Johnny said. "I hope she's worth it."

"She's worth more, but … I can't let her do this. He's a dangerous criminal. It ends today."

"I know people," Johnny reminded him. "I can call in the locals."

"Call a patrol car to take him away after I'm done with him," Aidan suggested.

"Ten-four," Johnny replied.

Aidan pulled up to the Hyatt valet stand, jumped out, and threw the keys to the attendant. "Aidan Castle. And I'm in a hurry."

The young man nodded. Aidan didn't give him a backward glance as he hurried into the building and headed straight to the alleyway leading to the famous Reunion Tower.

Checking his phone, he tracked Cara to the elevator and watched her get on. She wore jeans and a heavy black trench coat with her silver boots from last night.

Where were they meeting?

The restaurant?

He hit a button and waited. Fifty floors and sixty-eight

seconds. He kept repeating that in his head because he used to sneak over here and ride the elevator when he was a kid.

Could he make it in time?

Chapter Twenty

CARA'S HEART POUNDED as each floor of the elevator whizzed by. She'd managed to finally sneak away when everyone had gone to their separate rooms to gather their stuff before heading to Castle's to get dressed and dolled up.

They were probably just now missing her. She'd left a note in her room.

Errand to run. Will see you in the Castle's dressing room soon.

Her bridesmaid gown waited there for her, but she'd never get to wear it. She'd tried so hard not to ruin the wedding, yet now she would be doing that very thing. But … she couldn't let Trey get away with this. She'd find a way to stop him.

She had her tote bag with extra clothes and not much else. Not caring what Trey did now, she only wanted to get even with him and make him pay.

When she exited the elevator into the revolving, Asian-themed restaurant, her nerves surged into a rush of adrenaline. Trey sat at a corner table. He was just as handsome as she remembered, his dark blond hair thick and spiky, his icy blue gaze on her in that persuasive way she remembered so well. Yet, she felt nothing but disgust.

He stood as she approached. "Cara, you are as lovely as ever."

"Shut up and let's go."

"So anxious. Afraid your brother will come lurking?"

"No. I want this over with, and I want you out of my life. I'll miss my brother's wedding because of you."

"You missed our wedding, too, darling. Very bad form."

"I'm over being polite and following protocol, Trey," she said. "I'll only go with you under one condition."

"No conditions. You go or else."

"I won't go until you promise you won't involve Aidan in any of this. His name stays out of it. If you try anything more against my family or his—especially against him—after I give you this money, I will unleash the hounds of Hades on you. There will be no place on earth for you to hide."

Trey sank back in his chair. "You're in love with him."

"Yes, I am," she said. "But I'll let him go if you'll promise to leave him alone."

"You'd do that? Come with me even though you love him?"

"Yes. Now can we go?"

From behind her came a familiar voice. "Not so fast, princess."

Stomach in her throat, she spun on her heel to find Aidan standing not far away, a dark rage in his frown as he glared at Trey. "You need to understand something, Wellington. You're in Texas now. We do things our own way. Cara is not going anywhere with you."

Cara's heart almost burst with relief and love. He'd come

for her. He cared about her. "Aidan."

He held up a hand. "I told you to trust me. Did you honestly think I'd let you leave the country with this scumbag?"

"Did you honestly believe I'd actually go with him?" she retorted. "I had a plan."

"And just how do you plan on stopping me?" Trey asked haughtily, coming around to pull Cara close.

"I've already stopped you," Aidan replied. "Right now, all that money you've been bragging about in those dummy accounts is being transferred to another account that I've moved to a safe location. You might know of it. The Robin Hood account."

At that exact moment, Cara knew she would love Aidan Castle for the rest of her life. They stared into each other eyes, all forgiven.

Trey cursed, reached in his pocket, and pulled out a tiny handgun. In one desperate move, he jammed it into her ribs. "I'd stop that transfer if you want her to live."

AIDAN'S PULSE JUMPED into overdrive. He had people in place in case something like this happened, but he hadn't expected it here in a crowded restaurant.

Hiding the gun in the folds of Cara's coat, Trey moved her toward Aidan. "She's going with me. You are never going to see her again."

Aidan stared into Cara's eyes, seeing what lay between

them, the things they should have said to each other but couldn't. "I won't let that happen," he said to her and only her.

"How are you going to stop me?" Trey asked. "I can kill her right here."

"But you can't get away," Aidan said, keeping his voice even and calm. People were beginning to stare.

He needed a distraction, then realized he'd have one soon enough. While the swanky restaurant slowly revolved in a circle that offered panoramic views of the city, Aidan thought about all the ways this scenario could go.

"Come on," Trey said, impatient and in a visible panic. "Get out of the way. She's going with me."

Aidan sent Cara a warning glance.

"Are you going to hold that gun on me during the entire flight?" Cara asked, sending Trey a frown. "That is if we even make it through the airport."

"I'll handcuff you. Private plane."

She stayed calm, her eyes on Aidan while she talked to Trey. "You've got this all planned out, don't you?"

"I need your eyes and your fingerprints."

"But not me," she said, her gaze flashing back to Aidan. "You never really wanted me, did you, Trey?"

Trey pushed her forward. "None of that matters now."

Aidan stood between them and the elevator. "Wellington, don't do this. It's too late. The police are on their way."

Trey's calm slipped a little bit more as he came face to face with Aidan. "Do you want her to die?"

"You're bluffing," Cara said to Trey. "You have to know

you won't get past the lobby downstairs. This is over, Trey."

He frantically glanced around Aidan to where Johnny stood, holding an impressive-looking handgun on him. "Drop the weapon," Johnny said.

Trey grabbed Cara close, face feral as he shouted, "I will kill this woman if you don't let me out of here."

Aidan's heart did a downward spiral as he moved closer to Cara and Trey. "You're cornered, Wellington. You'll die before you can escape this building."

Wellington pushed Cara forward while Aidan held his breath.

And then everything happened at once. Cara lifted her dainty foot, then rammed a four-inch spiked boot heel into Trey's Italian loafer. When he screamed in pain, she managed to wrench free, then turned and continued to kick him with her pointy-toed boot, then started hitting him with her tote bag for good measure.

About that time, Tobias and Saul came around the big elevator bank, Claude rushing in from the other side of the circular restaurant with the manager on his heels. Thankfully, they had called ahead and warned the staff and the police that there might be a scene.

In true Texas style, Tobias had a lassoed rope. He swung it in the air, snapping it toward the screaming, now-flailing Trey. The rope caught and Tobias pulled hard, jerking him away from the brunt of Cara's tote. Saul and Claude took over, dragging the con man to his feet while he still screamed profanities.

Aidan lunged toward Cara, grabbing her out of the way.

She still aimed her tote toward the lassoed criminal, tears streaming down her face.

Aidan spun her to face him and caught her hands, holding her tight as he reassured her. "I've got you. Cara, I've got you. It's over."

It was bedlam around them—people running and yelling, cell phones up in the air recording the whole thing, and the police showing up to take over the scene.

And all the while, the restaurant kept revolving and the world kept turning.

While Aidan held Cara in his arms.

THE CLOCK SHOWED three in the afternoon by the time the commotion calmed down and the police had everyone's statements. They'd moved Aidan and Cara downstairs into the hotel's security offices for privacy. Johnny helped referee the questions and answers, but they were finally cleared to go.

"We'll follow up on Monday," Johnny's detective friend said in jaded, bored tone. "But with this attempted kidnapping and the information you've provided, I think we can safely say Trey Wellington won't be conning women for a long time to come."

"Not to mention the women who are now willing to come forward," Aidan reminded the detective. "I have a solid list."

"Send it," the man said, saluting them. "Have a good

time at the wedding."

Aidan shot a grateful smile at Johnny. "Go ahead. We'll be there soon."

Johnny gave them a wink before taking off.

"We don't have much time," Aidan said to Cara as he escorted her to the valet station via a back entrance. "Are you sure you can do this?"

"I won't miss my brother's wedding," she said.

"Cara?"

"I can't talk about any of it right now, Aidan. I want to make it to the wedding."

He left it at that, but wondered if by saving her, he'd also lost her.

AT FIVE-THIRTY IN the afternoon, two days before Christmas, Claude escorted Eleanor Castle up the aisle to marry Nico Lamon by White Rock Lake with the vista of downtown Dallas shimmering in the distance and the waning sun setting over the water. The white pelicans flocked in harmony, an added touch provided by nature.

Cara stood across from Aidan, her heart bursting with so much love she could barely breathe, her black wrap enveloping her in warmth. Eleanor looked every bit the princess in her full-skirted Lamon original wedding gown with sheer sleeves. She wore a white cape that Claude removed when she reached her groom, the warmth of glowing silver industrial heaters lighting up their faces as they smiled at each other.

The ceremony was over in ten minutes. Sweet and traditional, loving and beautiful. The bride and groom laughed and kissed as they moved toward the big tent for the reception.

Then the attendants followed.

Tiffany and her smiling husband Jasper along with their daughters, who'd been flower girls.

Johnny and Annabelle, holding each other close.

Aidan moved toward Cara, taking her arm in his. "How you are doing, princess?"

She sniffed away tears. "Better."

"I have so much to say to you," he whispered.

"I know."

They made it past the smiling guests along the path to the warmth of the big tent full of white lilies and red poinsettias, the tables ablaze with silver candles. But he stopped her by one of the Twelve Days of Christmas displays.

"I love you."

Cara's heart couldn't be any fuller than it was at this moment. "I love you, too."

"But do you trust me?"

"I do," she admitted. "I trusted you'd find me today, and you did."

Aidan dropped a kiss on her upswept hair. "You're with me now. Always."

"Always."

The rest would come out in the wash. But none of that could dampen this moment. All that mattered was she loved

Aidan and wanted a life with him.

In a haze of giddy relief and love, they danced and laughed and celebrated. Later, Claude came in and said, "Well, it's snowing. But we don't think it'll stick this time. Love sticks, but snow melts."

Everyone laughed at that.

Nico cut in on Aidan to dance with his sister. Smiling, he whispered in her ear, "Did I ever tell you why I chose you to run the Lamon Foundation?"

"No … why? Are you about to fire me?"

"Not at all. Why would I fire my Robin Hood who robbed the House of Lamon … but made sure the money went to people who needed it?"

"You knew all along?"

"I'm your older brother, and I'm responsible for all of us. Of course I knew. I also know you added money to the account and never spent a dime in it." He kissed her cheek. "I love you, little sister."

Aidan came back, raising an eyebrow with a grin. "Good talk?"

"Yes." She'd keep that conversation to herself for now. "I have a good brother."

"Will you be at the grand opening of my tech store?"

"Of course."

"Wear those killer shoes, will you?"

February 14th, the next year

AIDAN STOOD ON the balcony overlooking the VIP crowd on the floor below. He felt pride swelling in his heart. His store was a success, and he finally had a place of his own here in the world he knew best.

He only needed one more person here to make this night the best one of his life.

The front door opened and there she stood, wearing the required black and white. A sleek long-sleeved sheath, black but with tiny white pearls stitched all over the front all the way down, her hair upswept with a luscious sweep of bangs. Catching his eye, she pointed to her bootie shoes. Those shoes she'd worn to the rehearsal dinner, and then again on the day she'd pounded one of the stiletto heels into Trey's foot.

Killer.

A grin lighting her face, she moved through the crowd and up the stairs, never missing a step.

"My high-tech prince," she said before she kissed him.

"My bride," he replied. "Glad you're back from Europe, princess."

"I'm back, and I'm never running away again. I'm with you now, Aidan."

They gazed to where the people they loved stood holding champagne glasses in their honor.

Eleanor lifted her glass high, her smile serene as she took a microphone and said, "To think it all started with a shoe. The Castle legacy is intact. I thank all of you and love each of you. Always. To Castle's Department Store."

Everyone cheered, the music cranking up after Eleanor finished the speech. Toby Keith, of course.

Aidan leaned close to Cara. "And to the kissing theory."

Cara tugged him into her arms. "No longer a theory, darling. It's a fact." Lifting onto her tiptoes, she slanted her mouth over his in a deep kiss to prove it.

THE END

The Castles of Dallas Series

Castle Department Store is a downtown Dallas icon, but most of the elite shoppers who frequent the high-end store don't know the history of the beautiful mural in the shoe department. Come along with the Castle's to a world where glamorous high fashion and over-the-top romance brings about grand gestures and happily-ever-afters.

Book 1: *Undercover Princess*
Eleanor Castle's story

Book 2: *Lone Star Princess*
Annabelle Castle's story

Book 3: *The Runaway Princess Bride*
Aidan Castle's story

Available now at your favorite online retailer!

About the Author

Lenora Worth writes romance and romantic suspense for Love Inspired and also writes for Tule Publishing. Three of her books finaled in the ACFW Carol Awards and several have been RT Reviewer's Choice finalists. She also received the RT Romance Pioneer Award for Inspirational Fiction. "Logan's Child" won the 1998 Best Love Inspired for RT. She has made the NY Times, USA Today and Publishers Weekly bestseller lists. With eighty books published and millions in print, she enjoys adventures with her retired husband, Don. Lenora loves reading, baking and shopping … especially shoe shopping.

Visit her website at www.LenoraWorth.com

Thank you for reading

Runaway Princess Bride

If you enjoyed this book, you can find more from all our great authors at TulePublishing.com, or from your favorite online retailer.

TULE
PUBLISHING

Made in the USA
Coppell, TX
22 March 2023

14630948R00135